Permanent
Visitors

The

John

Simmons

Short

Fiction

Award

University of

Iowa Press

Iowa City

Kevin
Moffett

Permanent
Visitors

University of Iowa Press, Iowa City 52242

Copyright © 2006 by Kevin Moffett

http://www.uiowa.edu/uiowapress

The publication of this book was generously supported by the
National Endowment for the Arts.

The University of Iowa Press is a member of Green Press
Initiative and is committed to preserving natural resources.
Printed on acid-free paper

Library of Congress Cataloging-in-Publication Data
Moffett, Kevin, 1972–.
    Permanent visitors / Kevin Moffett.
        p.   cm.—(John Simmons short fiction award)
    Short stories.
    ISBN 0-87745-992-4 (pbk.)
    I. Title.   II. Series.
    PS3613.O365P47 2006
    813'.6—dc22   2006041802

06   07   08   09   10   P   5   4   3   2   1

for Corinna

Contents

ACKNOWLEDGMENTS

The following stories first appeared, some
in different form, in these publications:
"Tattooizm" in *Tin House*; "The Fortune
Teller" in *StoryQuarterly*; "The Medicine
Man" and "A Statement of Purpose" in
McSweeney's; "Space" in *The Chicago
Tribune*; and "Ursa, on Zoo Property and
Off" in *Bridge Magazine*.

I'd also like to thank the following people
for their advice, example, patience, prodding,
skepticism, and support: my family, Evaggelos
and Crista Vallianatos, Joan King, Peter Leon,
Eli Horowitz, M. M. M. Hayes, Rob Spillman,
Carol Ann Fitzgerald, Elizabeth Taylor, Mike
Newirth, Padgett Powell, James McPherson,
Josh Kendall, Deb West, Jan Zenisek, Connie
Brothers, Dan Gutstein, Austin Bunn, Matthew
Vollmer, Nic Brown, Andrew Friedman, Earle
McCartney, Holly Carver, George Saunders,
everyone at the University of Iowa Press, and
Jen Carlson.

And Ellis and Corinna.

Permanent
Visitors

Tattooizm

Dixon drives. Andrea attends to the beachside drifters pushing shopping carts along the sidewalk. She calls them "Cajuns." She likes how it sounds when yelled. Cajun! She likes that the drifters have no idea why she chooses this, of all things, to yell. She and Dixon drive past a restaurant that sells only hot dogs, past a giant rocking chair made of cockleshells, which you can pay to sit on. Cajun! Andrea wants to throw something. A ripe pear, a stuffed animal maybe, something not too hard.

Dixon is excited. He sings along with "Afternoon Delight" on the radio, smiling without smiling, something in the squint of his eyes. Andrea isn't bothered by his singing—his voice is soft, non-intrusive, nearly pleasant—but she finds herself waiting for him to stop. In a few hours she has to babysit for her brother. She thinks: *Something has always just happened or is about to happen. Nothing is ever* happening.

She is nineteen, Dixon, twenty-four. He has red, tightly curly hair, red eyelashes, red hair on his arms, his chest, red hair all over, except on the top part of his legs, which is shaved. He is training to be a tattoo artist by practicing on his thighs, covering them with flames, leaves, wings, cartoon characters, hearts, crosses, squiggles, spirals, and other meaningless designs. When she first met him there were freckles and soft red hair on his thighs. Now it's a mess, a tattoo stew. He is wearing shorts and if Andrea looked away from the street and at his right leg, she would see a purple tiger paw pulling scratch marks across his thigh.

A man pulling two clear plastic bags steps into the crosswalk. "Cajun!" Andrea yells. The man jerks his head forward, then sidelong like a fish extending for a worm, hooked.

He has to practice on somebody, Dixon tells her.

He is singing again, to a song that goes, "I want it," over and over—*it* being, Andrea guesses, sex. Dixon is excited because they are going to see a building he wants to turn into a tattoo studio. He drives exactly thirty-five miles an hour. He thinks the streetlights are timed so that if you maintain the speed limit you won't get any red lights. Every few blocks he's proven wrong.

Early this morning, they were naked in his bed. "Maybe you could allow me your right shoulder," Dixon said, tracing a finger along her clavicle. Andrea told him that at the end of August, on their first anniversary, she'd let him tattoo a small roman numeral *I* on her thigh. She's mad at herself for saying it. She doesn't want a small roman numeral *I* on her thigh. It seemed reasonable when they were naked. Anyway, it didn't satisfy Dixon at all. "I need practice," he told her. "I'm running out of room on my legs. All I've got is my arm."

They pull up next to a stucco two-storied shop with dry-rotted awnings and a FOR LEASE sign on the front door. It used to house, Andrea can read in the dust and sand collecting on the torn-off window stickers, the Fun Shack. The building looks slightly nonplussed, as if someone has just asked it a question.

"Look inside," Dixon says. "Imagine chairs and artwork on the walls. A big dog walking around." He sprints across the street, kneels to one knee, and holds a camera to his face. Andrea waits for the flash's wink, but it doesn't come. The sun is shining.

She cups her hands over her eyes and leans against a window: a pair of sawhorses, balled-up tarps, bar stools. The blond pine floor shines in parallelograms where the afternoon sun comes in through the windows. Andrea tries to imagine a big dog walking around.

"It's expensive," Dixon says when he gets back. "And the location is no good. We'll have to lure people down here."

She should offer something pleasant. She should compliment him on finding this Fun Shack. He is sitting on the hood of the car, deep green tattoos sneaking out of the hem of his shorts. "Tattooizm," he says. "There'll be an orange neon sign in the front window. Tattooizm with a Z, indicating impatience with the way things are."

She could say she likes the pine floors, that he has managed to find a building with the loveliest pine floors she's ever seen. "Aren't there licenses you need?" she asks. "How are you going to afford it?"

"Loans. Business loans."

"Didn't you ruin your credit, Dixon?"

"Come here and enjoy our building." He pats the hood of the car. It makes a solid, an unsociable sound. "Let me worry about the particulars."

She walks over and sits beside him. He reaches his hand inside the waistband of her shorts and underwear, rests it casually atop her thigh. Whenever she hears what kind of person Dixon thinks he is, it causes her to wonder what else he is mistaken about. Does he realize that lately he uses *we* when talking about his plans for the tattoo business, and that she feels pretty much indifferent to the whole thing?

His hand is just *sitting* on her thigh, inert as a cicada's vacated husk. Stillness unbothered by anticipation—it makes her jittery. She grips his elbow and moves his hand higher and to the right, closes her eyes while he maneuvers his fingers up, searching for her, slowly, finding her. He rubs with two fingers, rests his thumb in her navel.

Her new favorite answer when her next boyfriend asks what Dixon was like: He could draw a really good Yosemite Sam.

She looks forward to some rest when school starts in three months. Dixon's an increasingly demanding lover. In the morning he picks her up and they drive around or go to his house and have sex three, four times before she has to babysit her brother in the evening. Dixon lights candles, burns sage oil, turns his bedroom into a little shrine. He keeps his shirt off, his hair wet from repeated showers. They watch a lot of TV together: Dixon has a lot of channels. Sometimes while a woman in an apron, say, is extra praising a no-wipe oven cleaner, the TV goes black and Andrea looks over to see Dixon's rapt face moving toward her lap. She helps him slip off her underwear, leans back on the sofa, tunnels her fingers through his tight red curls. He has a certain appeal, she'll be the first to admit.

Now, on the hood of his car, she shudders from her tailbone ahead toward Dixon's hand. Once the feeling passes, she's left fogged by momentary cheerfulness. Dixon slowly slips his hand out of her shorts. Her eyes are closed. The sun backlights the blood vessels in her eyelids. She opens them and sees Dixon holding his hand aloft and still, like it's about to be fitted with a special glove. "Well," he says.

The air smells very suddenly like orange blossoms.

"It's a nice building," she says.

Dixon smiles, hops off the hood of the car. "I wish that expression were permanent. I wish it would stick around a few days at least."

"What are you talking about?"

He kneels, pulls the camera out of his pocket, and snaps a picture of her. "Satisfied. I've satisfied you."

She lets whatever expression was on her face go slack.

"And away it goes," he says. "Hope it sends me a postcard."

He drops her off at the security gate to the Grove, where she lives with her mother and brother, and where the guard has told Dixon that since his car is no doubt leaking oil, he can't drive in, where there are children and wading birds and endangered cypresses. The second he pulls away, Andrea feels untethered. Never has someone's absence exerted such influence on her.

When they're apart she is nagged by the certainty that she neglected to say the thing that would have set things right. She's been dishonest in her silence.

"We could live on the top floor," Dixon said as they were pulling into the Grove. Andrea was too surprised by the suggestion to laugh, which would have been the correct response. Whereas she imagines living above a tattoo parlor by the beach as akin to being nailed into an attic and having food passed to her through a slot, Dixon happily refuses to bother an idea like this past speculation. There was an old *Pennysaver* on the seat between them, and she should have rolled it up and swatted him across the chest or put it to his ear and yelled, "You aren't my future."

She's been out of school for more than a year. In the fall she begins classes at the junior college. She looks forward to paying attention again, to being rewarded for listening and remembering. She needs to buy folders and pens, some new clothes. Most people are unhappy about going to the junior college, but Andrea is not. Or she is, but only slightly. She is determined not to be.

Her little brother, Cory, meets her at the front door and tells her that their mother has already left for work. He begs Andrea to hurry taking off her shoes so they can microwave some nachos. Cory finds intense satisfaction in watching the cheese melt and bubble and congeal on the chips. He is part boy, part savage. Andrea wants to encourage the boy so she gladly microwaves the nachos. She gladly does any old moronic thing to make him happy.

She layers the chips in a collapsed-domino pattern on the platter. "We found a plumber," he says when Andrea asks how his day was. "Mommy cut my hair while I stood in the tub. We hanged another feeder."

Cory's hair looks exactly as it did last night: ragged around his ears and neck and pasted in a straight, straight line above his eyebrows. He has a barely kempt look to him, like a parolee on a job interview. A dubious boy's face has replaced the vacant infant's.

"You were gone when I woke up," he says. "Were you in school?"

Andrea opens a bag of pre-grated cheese. *Three Cheeses in One!* the bag says. "I haven't started yet, remember? I was out with a friend."

"Mommy says you want to marry a man from the circus."

Andrea pours the cheese over the chips. It comes out in three colors: white, orange, and very orange.

"The Human Sketch Pad," Cory says.

"She knew you'd tell me that," Andrea says, wiping her hands on the front of her shorts. "Mom thinks things are one way when really they're another."

"I thought she was gonna tell me a joke." He lays a hand on the platter. "Don't microwave them yet. I want them to be like this for a while."

Andrea misses childhood. Her childhood ended the morning she bled from her vagina, according to Miss Moten, her eighth-grade health teacher. Miss Moten also said that having sex was like being tickled from the inside out. One day in class she removed her shirt to demonstrate the correct way to apply deodorant. Some parents complained, but it turned out Miss Moten had obtained necessary clearance from the county to remove her shirt in class. Since then, things have gotten considerably less wondrous in Andrea's view. She supposes Miss Moten was more or less right about everything.

"Left side, right, middle, middle," Cory sings as the nachos cook. It's a song from a TV show which he's adapted for the nachos. Andrea touches the pause button on the microwave, and her brother shrieks with delight. When the nachos are sufficiently scorched, she dumps them into the garbage.

The phone rings while she and Cory are playing checkers with canned food on the kitchen's checkerboard linoleum floor. "The forearm," Dixon says, as if answering a trivia question, "is deceptively small." Andrea sits on the countertop with a dented can of butter beans in her lap. Cory has run off somewhere. "I just put a roman numeral *I* above my wrist. Wait till you see it. It's perfection."

Dixon is probably playing with himself. Often he does while they talk on the phone. He probably hasn't even taken off his surgical gloves. His penis is drooped like a sunburned mushroom out of the fly of his boxer shorts while he handles it carelessly, probably.

"What's your middle name?" he asks.

"Olive," she says, though this is not true. Her mother didn't give her a middle name.

"Spelled in the traditional way?"

"Don't put *Olive* on your arm, Dixon. Why can't we talk about normal things?"

"My arm, your middle name, we're talking about normal things." He sighs. "Listen, I took a nap when I got home and dreamt that you let me tattoo strings along your spine and an f-hole on each side of your back. When I made love to you from behind, it was like plucking a cello. I awoke and, well, I guess it goes without saying..."

Made love to you from behind, Andrea repeats to herself. It is perhaps the worst attempt at delicacy she's ever heard. She plans to tell her next boyfriend that Dixon had a foot-shaped gas pedal in his car. That he was fond of movies in which an adult and a child switch bodies. That he meant well, but emotionally he wasn't her equal. She's always been mature for her age. The next boyfriend will already have started to surmise this.

She tells Dixon she has to go find her brother.

"Sometimes," he concludes, "I think you and I are wilting from our own need."

Out back, Cory is refilling the new bird feeder. It's a test tube–shaped container with flower-shaped holes through which red liquid leaks onto the deck. Cory tears open a sugar packet and pours it into the feeder. "Mommy says that a hummingbird's tongue soaks up nectar like a paper towel with juice," he says. "Its tongue is shaped like a *W*."

How entirely beside the point! Andrea is too young to be smothered by Dixon's longing. He seemed so self-contained when she met him at the art-supply store. She was buying markers for Cory. Dixon was waiting for her, or someone like her, it's clear now. Someone who acted more experienced than she was. Someone who'd had sex maybe a dozen times with a surfer boy who, she's presently reminded, claimed he could tie a cherry stem into a knot with his tongue, but who broke up with her before he showed her, and who used to talk about Costa Rica, and who laid a Quiksilver towel over his bedspread before they began kissing.

"Squirrels are smarter than birds," Cory is saying. He walks around checking the other feeders, which are topped with wooden squirrels to deter real squirrels.

"I was having trouble finding anything I want in here," Dixon said when she met him at the art-supply store. "Are you an artist?"

Andrea will allow Dixon this summer. He had last fall, he has had winter and spring. Summer will be a nice end of the cycle. She will start college and meet nice boys with manageable obsessions. Of course she intends to remember Dixon fondly, like an old toy or a book that she read in bed when she was sick.

One day she wakes up thinking: *I am becoming what I wasn't.* It seems terribly ominous in the haze of sleep, but really it doesn't make much sense. Or it does make sense, but it's too obvious to think about. She isn't sure. Sex is draining her, turning her into a dull and contented cow. Away from Dixon, when she is able to consider, really stop to soberly consider, the physical act of sex, she decides it is overrated. Just because it feels good doesn't mean she should spend all day doing it! Soon it won't be special anymore. Dixon doesn't know anything. If he weren't around, she could easily be happy without having sex three, four times a day.

She misses her friends. She had just two: Jamie and Erin. Jamie was earnest and creative, and Erin was sarcastic and good with her hands. Both met Dixon once and said he was nice. Nice, even when Andrea barely knew Dixon, seemed wrong. Either they hated him or they weren't too perceptive. Jamie said he had a nice voice; Erin thought he was too skinny. Really, they thought he was old and weird and gross. Andrea has stopped calling her friends, because what's the point? She has stayed and they have left. Jamie is attending culinary school, and Erin plans to become a merchant marine. Andrea has no clue what, exactly, being a merchant marine involves, but she loves the sound of it. She is jealous of Erin. In ten years Erin will be able to say: *Back when I was a merchant marine . . .*

A substantial part of life, Andrea thinks, is finding and wanting things you like the sound of.

Dixon picks her up and they drive to his house, along the beachside. "Cajun!" Andrea yells at a woman reading a newspaper on a park bench. The woman looks up from the paper, and she isn't a drifter at all, just a normal woman with windblown hair.

"The junior college was on TV last night," Dixon says. "They asked some foreign students what they liked about the college and one of them said, 'Every day is discovery.'"

They drive past the deserted hotel's parking lot, where kids from the high school used to gather on weekends. A vinyl banner attached to a flagpole says PARDON OUR PROGRESS. Though Andrea never went to the parking lot, she feels nostalgic driving past. Mondays at school she would hear about fistfights and arrests in the parking lot. Once someone with a pitchfork threatened someone else.

"I've never been anywhere," Dixon says.

Andrea yells at a black man on roller skates carrying a rake and a pail. She's not sure why she has continued yelling at the drifters, she means them no harm. Their lives, she knows, are difficult enough without being yelled at by someone in a passing car. It is something she and Erin started doing in high school. Andrea would yell, "Cajun!" and Erin would yell, "Rubble!" It was very funny. They would never yell something overtly mean like "Bum!" or "Loser!" For starters, neither, when yelled, sounds as good as "rubble" or "Cajun." Probably it is the nicest sounding thing the drifters will hear yelled at them all day. Erin used to call the people who hung out in the deserted hotel's parking lot "combers," because the hotel was called the Beachcomber. Probably Andrea's nostalgic about the parking lot because she can't go there anymore, even if she wanted to, which she does not.

Later, naked in bed, Dixon strokes her thigh. Candles cast roving shadows on the walls: excited arms, retreating animals. Andrea watches the shadows and tries to discern a pattern, but there is no pattern. Dixon's sheets are sandy. His pillowcases smell like his scalp.

"Flex," he says. His hand, moving upward along her leg, stops on the crease of skin where thigh meets pubic bone. He rubs it. "Does that feel good?"

"Sort of," she says. "Not overly." In the candlelight, his forearm looks meticulously bruised, or gangrened. Andrea knows what is there: in the center, written in dark and elaborate cursive like a formal declaration, is Olive, followed by an exclamation mark. The *O* is set apart from the *L* so it looks like *O live!* The rest .

of the arm is beset by roman numerals, dozens of tiny *I*s and *X*s and *V*s scattered at random.

The lines on the new tattoos are more assured, the shading more delicate. Clearly he is improving his technique. But oh! Andrea cannot look at the new tattoos. They are indisputably, noisily, mistakenly about *her*—and permanent, permanent, permanent. She instead looks at Dixon's thighs, at the symbols that have nothing to do with her. She can look at the thighs without feeling anxious. The thighs, compared to the forearm, are Disneyland.

"Does that feel good?" he says.

Today in the gas station the cashier pointed to Dixon's arm and said, "Those aren't *real*, are they?"

Andrea thought this the worst response that one with tattoos could hope for, but Dixon seemed pleased by it, like he thinks he's defying reality or something.

He's still pleased. His face, lit from below by the candles, looks hollow and evangelical. He tucks his hand between the fleshy part of her thighs. "I want to fall asleep with my hand between your thighs," he says. "I won't pull it out till morning."

She has decided to break up with him on August 25, which will be a week before their first anniversary and one day before classes begin at the junior college. There is no way she's letting him touch her with the tattoo gun, which sits beneath a T-shirt on his nightstand, and looks nothing like a gun. It looks like a dart attached to an engine. "Tattoo *machine*," he says when she calls it a gun.

She has registered for four classes: Calculus, Argumentative Writing, Geology Lab, and Volleyball. They offer a class in volleyball! She is going to be polite and astute, the most hopeful student on campus. She plans to join clubs, form study groups. She'll volunteer to help deaf students take notes. She'll bring extra pens to class. She'll be reluctantly popular. She'll wear a sweatband and those cool little canvas knee pads to play volleyball.

Dixon goes to the kitchen, returns with a bowl of blackberries, and watches Andrea eat them. When she finishes, he puts the bowl on his nightstand. She rolls over onto her side and he rubs himself into her. She exhales a forced breath. He seizes her ear, her entire ear, with his mouth and gently bites the cartilage. It feels good. Almost everything he does to her feels good. He grips her hand, brings it around, and puts it between her legs. She touches herself but it seems a bit redundant, so she reaches behind and clutches his hip, which is sweaty. He is working hard. Her hand follows the thrust and pop of his hip. He whispers what sounds like *little tin pans*. The shadows on the ceiling have gone crazy. The sheets are still sandy. She makes long low sounds, smeared, overrun.

In the shower Dixon scrubs her back with a sponge. Her eyes are closed beneath the showerhead. The water is too hot, Dixon is scrubbing too hard, and for now everything is righteously okay.

While they towel off, he tells her he is taking her home early because he has an appointment to talk to someone about a work space.

"What's happening with the building?"

"A new plan," he says. "I haven't told you about our new plan?"

"You haven't told me about any plan."

"I guess that's because it's a *surprise* plan." His big laugh reveals a space between his canines, a word missing a letter. His chest, covered in freckles, is orangish from the hot water. "I'm doing research right now. But soon enough, this new plan is going to happen. Prepare yourself."

She thinks: *Soon enough a lot of things are going to happen.* The muscles in her nose twitch, like a rabbit nose. She sneezes.

As Dixon dries the top of his forearm gingerly, Andrea looks at his thigh, at a cluster of blue spheres above a semi truck hauling a bolt of lightning. Above the spheres, below a thicket of red hair, is his penis. It looks beleaguered. Andrea feels sorry for it. Flushed, crooked, not knowing what will happen next.

Dixon towels off her back. When he's done he says, "You are immaculate."

He drops her off at the entrance to the Grove. The security guard is new, but Dixon doesn't try to sneak past. Andrea's walk back to the apartment is nice—past gnarled oaks with osprey nests that look like steel wool—long enough to collect her thoughts but not so long that she starts to doubt them. She makes nachos for Cory. She sleeps. She hasn't seen her mom in days. Her mom leaves notes on tiny scraps of paper, tapes them to the front door: *Remember Cory's teeth.* And: *Get melon.* Before Cory and her mom are awake the next morning, Andrea leaves the house. Dixon picks her up at the security gate, his hair wet, new tattoos on his forearm. They go to the drugstore and buy condoms for Dixon and folders and pens for Andrea. She needs to buy a rock kit for her geology lab, but she wants to see if she likes the class first. They eat lunch in Dixon's bed. They watch TV again. They get naked again. They stay naked for hours.

Dixon sits on the edge of the bed with the tattoo gun. "This *I* looks like a *T*," he says. "*T* isn't a roman number."

A week goes by. Another week. Andrea has trouble keeping track of what day it is. Naked, everything is pretty much the same as the day before, and after.

Except: Dixon has stopped mentioning the anniversary tattoo. He's not any less physically attentive, but he hasn't mentioned that his forearm is now fully covered with tattoos. She appreciates the consideration. She appreciates it and is suspicious of it.

One day, on the way back to the Grove, she says, "I don't want a tattoo, Dixon. I know I told you I'd let you give me—"

"I know," he interrupts. "Nobody's going to give you something you don't want." He turns to the open window. Did he spit? His head lurched slightly as if he did. "We can't want what we don't want," he says.

She laughs without meaning to. He sounds so earnest, like their conversation really means something. She can tell she's disappointed him. She'll continue to disappoint him. "It's so fake!" Cory says. This is Cory the savage. Andrea sits next to him on the couch, beneath a Superman blanket, watching two wrestlers on television karate chop each other. The crowd cheers when the man in black tights karate chops the man in red tights, and boos when the man in red tights karate chops the man in black tights. Both men glisten with oil. The man in red tights jumps on the back of the man in black tights and pulls his chin from behind. The camera cuts to a Japanese man in a tuxedo running with a folding chair toward the ring. "All he has to do is wiggle his way free. And then—" Cory jabs his elbow upward.

The Japanese man swings the chair at the man in red tights but instead hits the man in black tights, who cringes and stands up. He and the Japanese man begin karate-chopping each other.

Beneath the Superman blanket, Andrea has slipped her hand into her shorts. She intended to scratch an itch on her thigh, but once she moved her hand the itch disappeared. Now she has begun playing with herself. She pulls the blanket higher on her shoulders and massages wet folds between her fingers. At first she didn't realize what she was doing, she was just rubbing herself without ambition, but now she realizes what she's doing.

"It's so fake!" Cory shouts, accidentally kicking her arm. "It's so retarded!"

Now the man in red tights is struggling with the referee, trying to prevent him from stopping the match. Andrea fingers herself more vigorously. She rubs side to side, moving just her fingers; the rest of her body is perfectly still. It is like typing a single letter. She watches Cory. His mouth is open in an expression of pure malevolent joy. Rarely does she imagine anything sexual when she plays with herself. *This feels nice,* she'll think. *This is pleasurable.* Dixon could be a thousand miles away, on a Pacific island, tattooing himself with a bird quill. The important thing is that Cory is happy — she loves even Cory the savage: this is what she is thinking, or feeling, while she watches him watch wrestling. She fingers herself fondly and more intently. Dixon could be in Iceland, in Greenland, encased in ice, grinning as if he's performing a public service . . .

She moans loudly, twice, before she thinks to suppress it. She tightens up and a shudder passes through her, unaided.

Opening her eyes, she sees Cory staring at her. "Are you gonna pass out?"

"I'm dizzy," she says. "I think I might have food poisoning."

She runs to the bathroom, locks the door, and pumps soap onto her hands. She squeezes them together under the running water until they hurt. She is frantic, crying. What was she doing? Why couldn't she have waited until she was alone? Dixon's torn some seal or protective covering or something, and now she can't control herself.

"Are you okay?" Cory says on the other side of the bathroom door. "Can I help you throw up?"

Andrea tells him she'll be all right. She lets the faucet run, sits on the toilet, and cries a little more. When she's done, she feels emptied, better. She decides to paint her toenails copper red. She collects all the supplies from the medicine cabinet and sets them in front of her. Applying the nail polish, she imagines she's being evaluated. She's careful. Her strokes are smooth, no streak marks, no polish, not a drop, on her cuticles. How efficient her technique! How not-ugly her toes! Another vision of Dixon: shirtless in his bedroom, squinting, aiming the needle to his arm.

August 25, she reminds herself. Then Calculus, Argumentative Writing, Geology Lab, Volleyball. Volleyball!

In the living room, Cory is watching *Xtreme Animal Challenge*, which shows footage of animals stalking, chasing, catching, and eating other animals. The host says, "Does anyone have some jelly? Because this gazelle is *toast*!" A gazelle, pulled down in mid-stride by some lions, folds onto itself like an empty sleeve.

Andrea sits down next to her brother, who watches the lion eat the gazelle. The lion tosses a hunk of flesh aside. "Picky, picky," the host says. Why does everything have to be so hostile and funny? When she was Cory's age, she used to watch a woman tell stories using a series of hand puppets. At the end of the show the woman would hold up a mirror, turn around, and say, "Magic Mirror, tell me today, are all my friends at home at play?"

"This is tedious," Andrea says. "Do you know what tedious is?"

Cory considers it for a second. "No. Do you know that there are some plants that will eat ground beef?"

Later, Dixon calls. He tells her to be ready in the morning for a surprise. For the rest of the night Andrea doesn't know what to do with herself. She reads a book to Cory who lies on the carpet with his eyes closed. She studies her toenails, which, dry, are more ruby red than copper red. Oh, the little disappointments. She imagines she is still being evaluated, but now she isn't doing so well. She's being penalized for diminishing congeniality. Dixon should know that saying get ready for a surprise makes the surprise unsurprising. There's still the surprise, but not the surprise of the surprise.

"Cory?" she says.

He has fallen asleep on the carpet. Asleep, he looks like Cory the boy again.

In the morning, when Andrea locks the front door and starts down the driveway, she sees Dixon's car coming up the street. It moves slowly and low to the ground, scurrying forward like a cockroach. When she gets in she sees that Dixon is wearing tan slacks and a striped shirt with a button-down collar. His hair is wet, he's clean-shaven. There are small red bumps along his jawline. "The guard let you in?" she asks.

"I replaced my oil pan. He said I'm free to enter and exit at my discretion."

Turning out of the Grove, Dixon salutes the security guard. Cuff links, Andrea notices. She wears a tank top and a pair of shorts with a bad waistband. She feels gloomy and slack, inadequately prepared for the day; on her way to the front gate is when she usually prepares. Dixon, in that outfit, is going to expect something from her, she is sure.

On the beachside, they pass a water park: chain-link fences around yellow slides named after natural disasters. The Typhoon, the Tsunami. The early morning sun casts everything in blushing light, peach and sea-foam green like a yard sale sofa. The hotels, the houses, the streets. Dixon is excited today, singing with the radio. He smiles by squinting. He drives exactly thirty-five miles an hour. Every few blocks he's proven wrong.

A bearded man at the street corner points accusingly at a newspaper machine, argues with it. "Cajun!" Andrea yells out the open window.

Dixon turns down the radio. "Don't do that. Not today."

"Why?"

"It's childish. Plus today's different."

As if for proof, he pulls into the parking lot of a two-storied cinder block motel with yellow doors and a yellow sign: Side-o-Sea Motel. He leaves the car running while he goes into the office. Suede loafers, Andrea notices. She imagines he's attempting a romantic gesture by dressing up and bringing her here. She feels sorry for him, for herself. Wedged into the dashboard is a picture of her sitting on the hood of the car, taken when they went to see the Fun Shack building. In the picture she appears pleased with herself, sloppily.

Their motel room is dark and cold with ugly, palm-patterned drapes closed across a sliding glass door which, presumably, looks out onto the ocean. The floor is silver terrazzo, polished to dullness. Dixon sets a duffel bag on one of the beds, unzips it, and pulls out gloves, towels, disinfectant, tubing, his tattoo gun.

"What are you doing?" she says. She looks at the door, at him, at the door again. The door isn't yellow on this side, but brown.

"Unpacking," he says.

He stands between her and the door. "What are *we* doing? With your tattoo gun."

"Tattoo *machine*," he says. He's tricked her! He reaches into the duffel bag again—twine? handcuffs?—and pulls out a flyer. TATTOOIZM ENTERPRIZES, it says at the top. She scans the rest of it: something about free demonstrations, something about a variety of designs available. She's relieved, though not totally relieved.

"Do you realize that there are people who want tattoos but can't afford them?"

"You're kidding."

"No."

"This is the surprise? Tattoos for the underprivileged?"

"Do I look like I'm kidding?"

No, he doesn't look like he's kidding.

There's a knock at the door. Dixon opens it, and a tentative-acting drifter enters holding the same flyer Andrea is holding. Andrea sits on the bed while Dixon negotiates with the drifter. The man wants the Mitsubishi logo tattooed on his upper arm, his favorite car is a Mitsubishi. Dixon needs a picture of the Mitsubishi logo. The man doesn't have one—maybe there's a Mitsubishi out in the parking lot? "Listen," Dixon says. "I'll do a nice yin-yang for you. The yin-yang's been around for several thousand years."

The man considers it for a moment, shrugs.

Dixon unbuttons his cuff links and rolls up his sleeves while the man sits down with a cough on the other bed. The man smells like spray paint and stale beer. Dixon wipes the man's arm with disinfectant, then carefully assembles his tattoo gun. Andrea turns on the TV, lies on her stomach, and gets very interested in a special about famous despots. No reason to leave now: the special has just started. Most despots, but not all, are failed students, it says. Most, not all, love dogs. Most, not all, worry about their height. The more Andrea learns about despots, the less historic her presence in the motel room feels. She relaxes. The man on the bed next to hers coughs a scuffed-leather cough.

"Did yours hurt like this?" he asks after a while. Andrea waits for Dixon's answer, then realizes the man is addressing her.

"I don't have any tattoos," she says.

"It feels like I'm being chewed. No, friends, I don't think I like this one bit."

Dixon bears down over him. When he's finished, his gloves are spotted with dark blood. He conceals the yin-yang under a bandage and throws the gloves onto the floor. "Drink plenty of water," he says. "In about four days, the yin-yang will start to itch: don't scratch it. A slap, a light slap, will suffice."

Andrea imagines a great fog lifting when she starts school. She'll tell her next boyfriend that Dixon was avid about his work. *So few have such passion!* she'll say. So few do. When Dixon concentrates he looks like a boy. She likes him most when he is concentrating, when his expression is guileless and imperturbable. He is sexiest when he's at his most unaware. She probably won't tell her next boyfriend this.

A woman knocks on the door and asks for a red rose on her shoulder. Dixon didn't bring any red ink, so she settles for a palm tree. The woman falls asleep while he's working. The next man, who wants the Marine Corps bulldog on his stomach, settles for a palm tree also. "The palm is our most sophisticated tree," Dixon says.

The man has a blue tear tattooed on his cheek. When he leaves, Dixon tells Andrea that the tear means he has killed someone.

A woman in a Jaguars sweat suit comes in and says, "I came for some praying hands, but there's a dude downstairs talking about his arm being manhandled."

"He had sensitive skin," Dixon says. "Why don't I give you a sample with white ink. If it hurts too much I can stop and no damage done."

"I don't want no half tattoo."

"It's not a tattoo," Dixon says. "It's the tattoo *feeling*."

A tan boy in flip-flops comes in with a picture of a flag with a blue stripe at the top and bottom. Dixon studies the picture while Andrea studies the boy's toes: the hair on them is blond, almost white. Around his right ankle is an inch-wide tan line from his surfboard leash. He's a surfer, Andrea's age. He is watching her. She turns back to the television.

Most despots, but not all, die in uniform.

"You're Andrea, right?" the boy says.

Andrea looks up from the television.

"You used to date Bobby. He's always talking about you."

Bobby was, is, the surfer. "What do you mean?" she says.

"Bobby, when he's talking, a lot of the time it's about you. Does that make sense? 'Andrea told me blah but she meant blah-blah.' 'Andrea acted like she didn't like anything.' Bobby can't figure you out."

"Bobby wasn't too observant. I like plenty of things."

"Yeah. I'll be sure to let him know I saw you here. In this motel room. Bobby and I are leaving for Costa Rica in a few weeks."

It seems unfair that, now that they aren't together, Bobby always talks about her. When they were together, Bobby always talked about Costa Rica. "Tell Bobby people aren't supposed to be figured out," she says.

Dixon, who's been staring at the picture, hands it back to the boy. "I'm here for the needy," he says.

The boy looks at Andrea, then at Dixon, and seems to swallow whatever retort he had. When he leaves, Dixon bolts the door and sits down next to Andrea while she watches the closing credits. She singles out the nice-sounding names: Mira, Sven, Lamar, Katya.

The boy is going to tell everyone she's unhappy, jealous of him and Bobby on their way to Costa Rica. "For a few thousand dollars it's possible to live like a sultan in Costa Rica," Bobby used to say. He said it with such greedy certainty. "Who wants to live like a sultan?" Andrea would ask. What does Costa Rica have to do with anything? She isn't unhappy. What makes her unhappy is the fact that the boy thinks she's unhappy.

She rolls over and lets Dixon kiss her. He tastes familiar. He rubs her hips, then scoots down on the bed and removes her shorts and underwear in a single tug. He takes off his shirt and kisses her breasts, her navel, strokes her neck with his left hand. *O live!* she sees. Really, the tattoos don't look that bad. The lines are assured, the shading delicate. At least he's passionate about something.

He turns off the TV and removes his pants.

"Let's lie here for a little while," she says. Since the episode with Cory, she has begun refusing sex once per day. One has to make rules, even arbitrary rules. Refusing sex usually means delaying it for forty-five minutes.

"Whatever you want," Dixon says. He lies on his back and puts his hand in his underwear, where it remains. "I'm exhausted," he says. "We've done some good! I mean, let's not rest on our laurels, but let's not fail to recognize obvious truths."

Her heart beats erratically. Given the right wording, she thinks Dixon could persuade her to get a tattoo, a very small one, on her ankle. She thinks she could be persuaded, given the right wording, to do just about anything.

"Tell me about Bobby," he says. "We know he's a surfer. And that he's on his way to Costa Rica with another surfer. That he spends all his time thinking about you, like I do."

"I barely remember him," she says. This is true, and also insufficient. Once, she had a conception of how she would describe him to her next boyfriend, but she's forgotten it. Dixon has never asked about him. She says, "He drank a lot of water."

Dixon adjusts himself. "Everyone's a mystery."

"He liked summer."

"Most do."

She feels sad. She has long suspected that, behind her back, people were reaching a consensus about her. Soon Bobby and his friends will agree on her past, present, and future unhappiness. Andrea will concede the past, concede the present, but she is *not* destined to be unhappy! She's just overly hopeful. When reality fails to meet expectation, she's disappointed! Isn't everyone?

"Can I satisfy you now?" Dixon asks.

Yes, she tells him.

As he bites her ear, there's another knock at the door. They lie still until they hear footsteps retreating.

Later, Dixon says, "I've been thinking, Andrea. You said you don't want a tattoo, but do you realize I can put one anywhere, on your armpit, on the inside of your lip?"

She doesn't know the wording she was thinking of earlier, but she knows this is not it. She tells him she doesn't want a tattoo.

"You start school in a few weeks," he says. "Then what? We spend less and less time together. You're tired all the time. I call you and you're in class or at the library, studying with Ashley and Chad. 'Can I take a message?' your mom says. But there is no message. I'll go out of my way to drive past the college, imagining you in class, raising your hand, asking questions just to ask questions, trying so hard. I never raised my hand. I'm not stupid. How can I convince you how happy I'd be if you'd allow me to put a tattoo on your thigh? A remembrance, a tribute, small?"

Her first impulse is to argue with the prediction, to tell him that her starting school doesn't mean they'll break up, who knows what will happen. She's annoyed. Partly by the assumption that she's so easily distractible, partly by the fact that she and Dixon have been imagining futures so similar.

"How bad will it hurt?" she asks.

He says he can put the tattoo on the back of her thigh, which will hurt less because there's so much fatty tissue. "No offense," he says. "It'll take twenty minutes, tops."

He stands up before she says anything, puts on his underwear and a pair of surgical gloves, and begins cleaning the ink tube in the sink. She looks at the bedside clock: two hours until she has to babysit Cory. Dixon in the daytime, Cory at night. She is being pulled from both ends. The other day Cory said, "If I got a tattoo, it would be a word only I knew the meaning of."

She lies on her stomach while Dixon sterilizes her leg. The cloth is cool, and then the gun buzzes, and her thigh feels slightly hot, but she can see Dixon hasn't started yet. He stares at her thigh. "I can do a letter, a shape, anything you want."

"Where are you going to put it?"

"I'll center it. It'll look like it's been there all your life."

She tells him to give her a small asterisk on the side of her thigh, then explains what an asterisk looks like. Dixon nods, still staring at her thigh, memorizing it. He is excited. Andrea feels buoyed by his excitement. Finding the right things to want is easy, she decides. Actually wanting them, this is the difficult part.

She stares at the ugly drapes, waits for the needle. She thinks, *It's just as easy to make drapes pretty as drapes ugly.* She thinks, *Another contented cow thought.*

August 25. Calculus, Argumentative Writing, Geology Lab, and Volleyball. She'll get to know her professors. She'll buy terry cloth running shorts, a shirt with stripes down the sleeves. She'll befriend people because of their interesting-sounding names. She'll take notes with one of those four-color ink pens, changing ink color for each class.

Dixon dabs at her leg with a towel. He is leaning over her so purposefully, attending to her. "Almost there," he says. "You all right?"

She'll miss Dixon, she already misses him. The fog will lift and Dixon will be gone and she will miss him. She will tell her next boyfriend that Dixon, poor Dixon, was very nice, that she has nothing but nice things to say about him. The next boyfriend will understand. He will offer to scratch her back, or apply lotion to her back, or whatever the occasion calls for.

Dixon dabs at her thigh some more, then sets the tattoo gun on the end table. "I'm finished," he says.

"That's it?" Andrea says. "That didn't feel like being chewed."

"Fatty tissue," he says.

"Can I look at it. What's it look like?"

"It's lovely. A perfect souvenir."

She walks over to the full-length mirror. In her bare feet, over the dull terrazzo.

"It didn't feel like anything," she says. She turns around and looks for the tattoo. In the center of her thigh are a few beads of blood around a colorless star, a tiny patch of skin faded to white.

Dixon removes his gloves. They snap off his fingers.

"It isn't," he says.

The
Fortune
Teller

Long after the tourists stopped coming to her for advice, the fortune teller decided to stop offering it. She closed her shop, but continued paying rent while she figured out what to do next. Once in a while she would sweep the sand from the promenade in front of the shop, drag a padded stool under the canvas sunshade, and post herself there for a few hours, gazing out at the dim Atlantic. The ocean was where life started and where life would end. Sandpipers in unstated formations skittered by with impossible speed, rummaging the shallows. She had no close friends or family. Everyone she was familiar with had died, most recently M. E. Chaddock, six months ago. The fortune teller said their names when she bicycled past their old houses, herself still flush with rude health, pedaling down the sand-bleached sidewalks of the oceanfront on which she had lived so long. Her friends had left scorched patches all over town, holes she might tumble into if careless. She was calm, she was patient, but she had begun to foresee all kinds of calamity for the tenants of this world, and the fact that no one was sensible enough to seek her counsel saddened her.

She ordered fried clams and a nonalcoholic beer at a seafood place called Walkin' Charlie's, with hammocks and cast nets lodged with conch shells and nautiluses on the walls. The waiters glowed tan in the strangely lit restaurant and showed their teeth when they passed one another. The fortune teller's waiter had a tattoo of barbed wire twining around his bicep, and she asked him if the bicep was somehow dangerous or off-limits, and he stared at her for a few seconds as if at a magic trick poorly done, before asking if she needed another beer.

A dozen or so lifeguards in yellow canvas shorts tramped past her table to the bar. Their rowdy entrance upset the inertia that had settled over the little dining room which the fortune teller was just beginning to notice and enjoy.

"Buy Tito a drink!" one of them said. "Tito saved a woman from drowning today!"

She laid a napkin over the fried clams, congealing in their brown plastic basket. She had advised state representatives, police departments, a popular reggae musician! Confidential information had been entrusted to her; compromises were struck, special security clearances obtained in order to solicit her expertise. Hers was an ancient craft, not inherited but learned, based on the motion and subtle alignment of bodies. Most events preannounced themselves uncomplicatedly enough, one only needed to be patient and take notice. Toward the end, the fortune teller had begun lying to the tourists, predicting sunny expansive futures for them while, looking into their faces, she saw only disharmony and a vague tapering-out. They were bored. A fortune teller dealt in indefinite successions, carefully composed implication; what they wanted was a T-shirt or a shot glass saying they'd been to a seaside fortune teller. All she could offer them was remembrance of an unsettled future, and no one seemed interested anymore in unsettled futures.

The lifeguards sat crowded together at the bar, two deep, like eggs in a carton. Their cumbersome mirth, the pushy way they coronated their friend . . .

The fortune teller waited for the check.

She bicycled past M. E. Chaddock's old house, a few hundred feet from the beach, behind Lé Motel. Stacked cinder blocks under a red Spanish-tile roof, with twin porches, one on either side, suggesting barnacles, or parasites, something draining vitality from the house itself. The fortune teller had always liked the porches' jalousie windows, which opened outward by slowly turning a polished metal dial. The rear windows opened to reveal a swimming pool, to her an impossible luxury so close to the ocean, the front windows to a combed sand yard, which had been replaced, the fortune teller noticed as she bicycled past, with a graph of sod plots, coming up at the corners here and there like an old quilt.

"Margaret Emerson Chaddock," she said, pedaling by. "Collector of miniature bells."

She had intended to disremember where M. E. was buried so she could stop visiting her, but the name, Loblolly Gardens, refused to dismiss itself from her mind, although it wasn't clear to her what a loblolly was. The cemetery was too far to bicycle to, so she rode the bus there, transferring twice. She sat behind the drivers, offering questions if they appeared friendly. One driver she recognized from previous trips. He had a small grief-set mouth saved by warmly intelligent eyes behind bifocals that glanced at her every so often from the rearview mirror.

"Do you drive the same path every day?" the fortune teller asked him.

"No, ma'am," the driver said. "We alternate. In the morning they hand me a printout telling me what bus and route I've been assigned for the day."

"And you drive around and around in a circle all day long?"

"That's right. Actually, in a rectangle. I don't mind it, if you're worried."

The fortune teller pulled the cable and the driver stopped the bus, lowered the front end with a sustained hydraulic sigh, and as she debarked in front of the cemetery, he said, "Don't talk to no ghosts," in a way that made her pause, half-turning there on the corrugated stairs: not a warning or a judgment but one of a thousand offhand remarks that demanded no more acknowledgment from her than a smile. So she smiled.

At home, she washed black soot off her hands. She wasn't sure where it came from, the bus or the cemetery, but whenever she returned from Loblolly Gardens, her hands were covered with it. Outside the kitchen window, a seagull pecked stubbornly at one of the empty cans of cat food the fortune teller had left on the ledge. Across the alleyway, a single long tubesock was draped over her neighbor's porch railing, dirt-side up like a singed tongue. Everything can't be tragic at once, she thought. Breezes move in all directions, the bases of even the deepest holes sometime see the sun . . .

She opened a nonalcoholic beer and cleared a space for herself at the kitchen table. On a cocktail napkin she wrote, *I want to be put in the ocean*, watching each letter bloom as the black ink drowsed into the cotton. Not satisfied, she found another napkin and wrote, *It is my final wish that I be put to rest in the ocean*. She initialed it and taped it to the refrigerator.

They marked friends, mothers, veterans, husbands, daughters. One was littered with arcane tokens: marbles, wallet-sized photographs, plastic toys, combs, stones, seashells, a checkerboard, goggles, foreign coins. On one was a pastel Easter basket with a greeting card envelope inside, signed and sealed. Granite saints and angels adorned some of them, lazily peering down onto grass that was sharply, profanely green. One bore the inscription *Loved*

Horses. Another: *Could Carry A Tune.* The more recent ones showed color photographs of the dead and were equipped with flower clasps, most of them fastened around plastic bouquets.

The older ones, in a separate, less-tended lot across the street, were more austere. Names and dates, maybe a line of borrowed verse. A lot of children here, nine- and twelve-year-olds with first names like Elbert and Constance. The headstones had raised lettering—unlike those across the street which were incised—and, on many, all or part of the writing was beyond legibility. Only these heartened the fortune teller. She had walked across the street, stepping over the irregular ground, past the aspirin-white markers whose surfaces seemed to have been bleached by the sun, toward these older, tree-shaded ones, on whose surfaces age and dampness had obscured the inscriptions. She absently ran her hand along the cold, coarse tops of the mildewed markers as she read the half-messages:

Charles Th
Born

His memorial nearly erased from this world, Charles Th could soon safely roam the other, or disappear, or be invented again, far from Loblolly Gardens. The fortune teller thought *loblolly* might mean to wait. Anyway, it was a fine-sounding word, one she wished she had come across earlier. "Care to loblolly while I finish up?" she said to herself, patting the mold-blackened markers. "I'm not going to be loblollying here much longer."

She looked past the insolent grave markers, across the street at the outdoor mausoleum, U-shaped like a handball court, where M. E. Chaddock, fifth row, twenty-sixth column, a sturdy stamped bronze plaque at her feet, loblollied to be forgotten.

She won at jai alai, or the players on whom she bet won. They wore white vinyl warm-up suits distinguishable by varying neon stripes and polygons, and played behind a two-story-high glass wall. Finished with a match, they sat in the front row whispering in Spanish to one another as they watched the next group play. All of them, so wiry and sedate, carried the great kinetic stillness of athletes at rest. The few people in the fronton whispered during matches like the finished players, so the fortune teller could hear the pelota's *whiff* as it left the cesta and caromed off the wall. During intermission she cashed in her tote cards and ordered a real beer at the bar, savoring it for a while. The Star Spangled Banner played from an unseen loudspeaker and several people stood up, held their chests, and looked uneasily around the room, until one of them pointed to a television, which showed footage of a rippling flag. The fortune teller watched the bartender polish the beer taps with a blue rag. An animated young man with unkempt beetle-black eyebrows and wiry hair, he stood back from his work and regarded it with an irked frown, then, stepping forward again, finished off the taps with his shirtsleeve. When he was done, he said to the fortune teller, "I think these taps are clean enough to dispense you a free beer." He poured the beer and put it in front of her.

"You were born in the wrong time," she said. "These days a good boy is an unusual thing to be."

"Every time you come here you say that to me."

"But do you suspect I'm right?"

"Are you a gypsy or something?"

"No, I'm just tan and old."

"It's all how you feel, right?"

"Lately I feel old."

She rode her bicycle on the rutted sidewalk, cars passing by and disappearing one by one into a distant vista. The concrete of the sidewalk swelled and contracted, which was why it was rutted with gaps, wider in the winter than in the summer, and why the sound of her bicycle on it changed with the weather, now a less prominent tat-tat-tat-tat because it was warm outside. A long time ago, her great-uncle had taught her to pay careful attention to the subtle way things moved and aligned themselves. He told her to remember that she, too, was in motion, and not to falsely inhabit what she observed. The sun traveled above and below the equator in a year-long figure-eight only because the world was tilted; seen from a moving boat, the shoreline zoomed by. Her great-uncle had been a scientist or an inventor or doctor. He trapped rabbits and kept them in unpainted hutches as pets. She couldn't remember anything else about him. Maybe she had made him up. As she bicycled home from jai alai, the wind blew her hair out of its clip, or her own forward movement blew it out, and twice she had to pull over to readjust it.

She rode by M. E. Chaddock's again and saw that in the front yard an Open House sign had been stuck into the quilted sod. A small group of people had gathered at the front door which was, sure enough, open. The fortune teller steered into the parking lot of Lé Motel, gently gripping the hand brake as she turned around.

A woman with the small muddy eyes of a crayfish approached the fortune teller as she walked into the foyer. The house smelled like cookies.

"What a great time to buy," the woman said.

"I am here," the fortune teller said, staring down at the terrazzo floor, which was flecked with little gold and black galaxies. Unable to think of anything casual or sensible to say to the woman, the fortune teller walked on, down the hallway into the living room.

It surprised her to see the living room intact, more or less as M. E. had left it when she died six months ago. Four white wicker couches arranged in an open-cornered atoll with a card table in the center. M. E. had loved to play bridge when they were younger. She had been a serious competitor, unlike the fortune teller, and could spend hours among friends in silent concentration, thin cupcake-paper nicks forming above her top lip. The fortune teller noticed newly added flourishes in the living room suggesting a foolish chic M. E. never had. Vases of oleander clippings, an open parasol hiding the front of the fireplace, a painted conch shell resting on an array of magazines, one of them asking the fortune teller, *Do You Hate Your Problem Toes?*

On the porch, a woman had taken off her belt and was leaning against the window to measure the frames with it. The fortune teller waited for her to leave, then went to the windows and slowly turned the metal dial, watching the rear slats open to reveal the pool in the backyard. A swimming pool with the beach so close! M. E. was not the fortune teller's favorite friend. She could be mean and petty at times. She bragged too much about her son, a local bail bondsman who appeared in TV commercials. Someone should have let her know that her son looked walleyed on television, because he did. And M. E. herself had never been very pretty, never very pretty at all. Alone on the porch, the fortune teller tried to sew up her grief, for she could feel her eyes beginning to burn as she looked out at the swimming pool, at a boy who straddled the diving board, dipping his toes into the green water. The pool of her last friend, the last of the outlasted.

She went into the bedroom and looked for M. E.'s display case. The bed was made up with a new comforter, still creased where it had been folded in its packaging, and next to the bed, instead of the case, was a nightstand on which sat a cordless telephone and a jar of marbles. She found the case in the bedroom closet, covered up with M. E.'s bedspread, which years ago M. E. had embroidered with a large MEC on the right side and TKC, her husband's initials, on the left, marking where each of them slept. The display case held her collection of miniature bells, about fifty of them, souvenirs from years of summer travel and family vacations. The fortune teller kneeled down, opened the case, and brought out a bell made of crystal, with sea oats etched into it, her favorite. Holding the bell out in front of her, she gently chimed it—a clear uncomplicated sound. She chimed it again, then quieted it with her hand. It was what she imagined a summons from a newer world would sound like.

"Yoo-hoo," she heard the realtor call out from the hallway. The fortune teller stood up and closed the case. She left the closet, putting the crystal bell in her shirt pocket.

"Did you get a load of all that closet space in the master bedroom?" the realtor said as the fortune teller hurried by. "Every woman's dream!"

Sitting in front of her shop, she watched a group of teenage boys conferring with a punching machine at the arcade a few doors down. The machine, which was new, measured a puncher's strength, and attracted a particular sort of customer, the fortune teller noticed, one keen on having the strength of his punch measured, for starters. She recognized this particular group, one of the many who prowled the boardwalk afternoon and night, their bare chests exposed, arms and shoulders tattooed with various emblems. One had an ornate scene on the whole of his back involving skulls and bats; another had a sleeve of solid black, elbow to wrist; still others, initials on a shoulder, cartoons, names, symbols, patterns, crosses, designs made to look like flayed skin and the green scalloped hide of alligators. Each boy's body a careless remembrance to itself. They formed a V behind the puncher, who was negotiating the punching bag. One said, "Tasty cat! Tasty cat!"

The puncher took a few steps back, half-skipped toward the machine, and struck the bag, which seemed to slam into its slot before the boy hit it, as if anticipating the blow. Sirens sounded, horns and bells and blinking blue lights signaling that here was an illustrious puncher.

"Tasty cat!" the boy repeated.

The fortune teller, sitting about a hundred feet from the group, considered that he may not have been saying that at all. When a tattooed body expires, the fortune teller thought, its remembrance expires as well. Nowhere else for it to go. Down on the beach, the parallel tilted tops of umbrellas meant late afternoon, her storefront casting a long shadow in front of her on the promenade sidewalk, pelican silhouettes. When the ocean was serene, the fortune teller was serene, and today the ocean was serene. The small, glassy waves, four, five, six to a set, came to shore in orderly swells. They were pounding the shells to pieces, pieces to tinier shards, shards to sand. The sand stayed sand. You could taste it in the seawater when it got into your lungs, undissolved and briny like the water above. The thought of it made the fortune teller thirsty. She loved the ocean, but hadn't stepped foot in it for over thirty years. The more she had gazed at it from the front of her shop, the more ludicrous the idea of swimming in it seemed, like trying to inhabit a mural, or another person's sleep.

The tattooed boys had started arguing with one another at the punching machine, but this, the fortune teller noticed, was a new group of boys, a new group of tattoos. The other tattooed boys had moved on.

For now the crystal bell would rest on her kitchen windowsill. She had considered bringing it to Loblolly Gardens to leave on the ground in front of M. E.'s marker, but there were hundreds of other people in the mausoleum, and how would it be clear that the bell was for the one in the fifth row, twenty-sixth column? What if a careless mourner stepped on it, or someone stole it? Both, the fortune teller knew, poor excuses; nevertheless, they sufficed to keep her away from Loblolly Gardens for a few weeks. And, while she tried not to scrutinize too closely, she knew no one cared about the bells anymore, except her. A year ago they were M. E.'s beloved souvenirs from a life of vacations and travel, which she had asked her bail bondsman son to move into her bedroom when she got sick, so she would be able to take them out and look at them, ringing one of the bigger ones when the fortune teller walked into the house, letting her know that she, M. E., was in her bedroom. Today the bells were just odd relics in a display case, pushed into the spacious closet of the master bedroom of a house for sale. That is, if the bail bondsman hadn't carted them off to a thrift store by now, saving the silver and gold ones to trade at a pawn shop for a gas grill or a crossbow.

After putting cans of food on the window ledge, the fortune teller rang the crystal bell to call the neighborhood cats. In a few minutes the usual customers arrived: three well-fed-looking long-hairs and a short-hair with a lame front paw, all of them solid black. The fortune teller stood at the sink and watched them leisurely eat up the food. They seemed to work together, the long-hairs making sure the lame one didn't go unfed, pausing after they were done to lick themselves, unaware of the gray-haired intruder at the window, this seaside witch. But lately she haunted, with her raggedy troop of black cats, no one but herself. If a witch was indeed what she had been, her strengths had surely vacated her, like a hermit crab moving on to another shell when its old one became chipped or didn't suit it anymore.

She sat down at the kitchen table and wrote on a cocktail napkin: *It is my wish for all my personal belongings to be put*—

A few months ago, while sitting in front of her shop, she had had the idea of riding her bicycle straight into the sea. Just pedaling on in the shallow water between waves, deeper, downward along the ocean floor for as long as she could stand it, her hair sprouting out of its clip, her lungs filling with the sandy water.

She threw away the napkin and, on another, wrote, *I was a witch. All of my personal belongings should be burned at dawn*, which she initialed and taped to the refrigerator, just above the other one.

The idea of someone finding these remnants of her after she was gone suddenly made her smile. "Here we go," he would say, taking the two napkins in hand. She pictured a fireman, somebody with a heavy uniform and qualified concern. "Burn the belongings at dawn and put her to rest in the ocean. Fair enough."

———

The shop's lease expired in eight months. And then, someone would rent the space and use it to sell towels, tote bags, bathing suits, swim goggles, umbrellas, suntan oil, necklaces, picture postcards, shells, bits of coral, sunglasses, shot glasses, T-shirts. Or a whole shop full of punching machines, everyone standing around waiting to learn the strength of his blows.

For now, the fortune teller would come and sweep away the sand that had blown up from the beach onto the promenade sidewalk. The summer nearly over, tourists would walk past the shop, a few hesitating to consider the handwritten *Fortunes Told* sign before moving on, to the boardwalk, back to their hotel rooms. Each moved with contrary perpetual intent. One, a deeply sunburned woman in a bathing suit and purple sarong, her hair dripping with water as if she had just stepped from the sea, approached the fortune teller in front of her shop.

"I can't believe you're still here!" the woman said. "Thirty years ago you read my fortune when I was on Spring Break. Even your sign hasn't changed."

The fortune teller had been sitting on the stool and gazing at the ocean again. She had been wondering if a bicycle would sink or float, if the rubber tires were enough to bring a bicycle to the surface, or if the metal frame and handlebars would keep it below water, at rest on the sea floor. "What did I tell you thirty years ago?" she said.

"Well, I was born with a very potent forward tendency, was what you called it, and you said I would soon be entering a world of negative movement. All around, objects would try to depend on *me* for direction. It would be very difficult, but my forward tendency, you said, would carry me through. I would need to rely on neutral suspension, which you told me all about. And you said I would marry a Libra."

"And then?"

"That I would come here again one day and have my fortune read. You're very talented, everything happened just as you predicted."

A boy in socks ran by, carrying a pair of in-line skates. Close up, the woman in the sarong smelled like aloe, a damply opaque scent. Forward tendencies were the pretty ones, college girls with blonde hair and big, agreeing blue eyes. The fortune teller wondered what she would say when the woman asked for another reading. Would she take the woman into the shop and render for her a slow sunny descent? The exuberance of the thirty-year-old fortune unsettled her only a little. She had forgotten about neutral suspension: the ability to delay anticipation by expecting all outcomes, best and worst. An arcane formula, one of the many the fortune teller had once invented and sold as provisions against unsettled futures. The woman in the sarong was shaking her head, looking out at the water with the fortune teller.

"The ocean looks so calm," the woman said. "I'm glad everything is exactly like I remembered."

The fortune teller didn't have the chance to let her know that she no longer told fortunes. The woman had slipped off, back down to the beach. She didn't want her fortune read after all. The fortune teller saw her as a dim silhouette, standing barefoot in the shallow water. Though the sarong made her look wealthy and a little exotic, the sunburn meant careless, imprudent. The fortune teller predicted the woman would move into the deeper water at any moment. *Now*. No, *now*. She slapped at the little waves as she waded in, knee-deep, waist-deep. *Now*.

Ends usually preannounced themselves with one final alignment, a slight corrective sway, hardly noticeable. The fortune teller waited.

The
Medicine
Man

When I'm low, I go to Bel Air Plaza to look for the medicine man, Broom. He's not a medicine man in the exact sense, the ordained by his fellow tribesmen sense, but a generally wizened hard-looking Seminole Indian who works crushing boxes and sweeping, called Broom, you see, which I figure is more nasty than honorary, like the old Russians in the building where I live call me Florida Power because sometimes I wear a hat that says Florida Power. Crushing boxes and sweeping is no proper vocation for a medicine man, even nonordained from a tribe that isn't officially recognized as a tribe. Early in school you're taught Seminole is the only tribe to never officially surrender to the U.S. government and the only to help runaway slaves escape from crackers, which is whites with whips. My sister's husband says I'm manic depressant because sometimes I feel low and sometimes, like currently, high, and I think Indians are party to powerful secret forces even if they themselves aren't aware of it, like Broom isn't aware of it.

I didn't used to be so low-high. As a kid I played all the made-up games with my sister, Sally, games I can't recall now though I recall learning the rules, which varied from game to game, and now just to think about them, the rules, causes me, like it never used to, a certain quickness. Sally remembers the games and the rules to the games. Sally was a nice kid and is still nice. Maybe it's the games we played that made me low-high, or the rules to the games, which continued when the games ended, and often *became* the games, and continue now. Does anyone else feel a little pride to hear sirens and pull over to the roadside to let an ambulance or a police car pass by? It calms me.

Walking does too, especially mornings before the recycling truck comes, the blue bins curbed and filled with beer bottles, wine bottles, soup cans, leaflets, newspapers, antennas, half-and-half cartons, test tubes, magazines, cereal boxes, toothpastes. All this out in the open, this suggestion, to me it's like looking into people's secrets.

And visiting Sally, my sister, who lives in a condo at the beach with her husband, Steve, who teaches study skills at Flagler College. They're getting ready to have a baby, and what I really want to tell you about is the earphones and Sally's stomach, but I need to tell you first about Broom the medicine man, which I started to. He's who I was looking for before going to Sally's condo and seeing her with the conductant jelly on her stomach and the earphones which I put on while Steve said, *Do either of you have a goddamn*—but not yet, not yet.

Broom. Everyone knows you're supposed to bring a gift when you consult a medicine man, something valuable to you but not him so he can throw it away without regret. When I went to see Broom I had been low for almost six days. A thing happened at Indigo Pines, where I live with old people who're Russian Jews, escaped communists or escaped from the communists, they won't tell me which. These escaped Russians are old, old. I used to say I love all people, before these Russians, but now I can't. Now I love only most people, and I've started to suspect that once you start decreasing a thing it's easy to keep going. I'm allowed to live at Indigo Pines even though I'm not old or Russian or sick or ready to be.

Indigo Pines prints the menus in both Russian and English, and they're set in two stacks on a table in front of the cafeteria before it opens for dinner. I was early. I could smell it was zucchini latkes, that mossy smell zucchini latkes have, and I sat down and read the menu next to three Russians who are always sitting on the purple loveseat in front of the cafeteria, talking Russian or playing a Russian game with wooden pegs in a triangle, which is what they were doing tonight. The dinner menu said zucchini latkes with provençal sauce, which is spaghetti sauce, and at the bottom of the menu inside the Dinner Events box I read, Tonight is Indigo Pines Poetry Night! Between dinner and dessert, we will be passing out words and you will surprise us with your creativity! Should be fun!

When I read that, why didn't I leave and go to Hogan's Heros for an eight-inch number seven, no mustard, no lettuce, pressed, and watch them playing shuffleboard on that long tabletop with sawdust and spinny silver pucks, and eat alone but not lonesome with the noisy TV noise and eager people-standing-around-the-shuffleboard-table noise? Hogan's serves mugs of beer and sandwiches called heros which you order by number. I once overheard a woman there say she wanted no hot peckers on her hero and she meant, I've thought about it, hot peppers. Number seven means ham.

Being low-high causes bad decisions. I stayed at Indigo Pines for zucchini latkes with the thirty or so Russians who sat at the white-nylon-tableclothed tables in the same groups of five and six I'm familiar with and ate and talked Russian while I ate my latkes alone, and lonesome. Two Russians across the table from me gestured like weightlifters and laughed. I was wondering about *passing out words* by repeating it to myself while eating my latkes. The more I repeated *passing out words,* the more it sounded like something I might want to stay around for and I started to get excited, high. Plus, dessert was fruit blintzes which is like pancakes and good.

Passing out words meant being given a plastic ziplock filled with white pieces of paper with words typed on them. The Russians in charge of Poetry Night were young Russians. They cleared away my plate, leaving a fork for the blintzes, and then handed me a ziplock. One of them said, Take a few minutes and make a poem. Remember, one sentence is all it takes to surprise us with your creativity! And so on. The young Russians who work at Indigo Pines are pale and have bright blue eyes like huskies. They're a little nicer than the old Russians but still not nice.

My ziplock was stapled shut, and I opened it and put all my words on the white tablecloth in front of me with a few flower-formed stains from the provençal sauce. My words were: On Some For Time The What And Mister Blew If. I was trying to figure out the rules of the game, what was expected of me to make this poem out of these words, who I would surprise with what, and why. I raised my hand to try to get the attention of one of the young Russians in charge of Poetry Night to tell them I wanted a new ziplock of words, these are poor words I was going to tell them, but they, the Russians, the young Russians—all these Russians in Florida!—were gone. The quickness. Like being sped up and slowed down at the same time. These *words*.

I tried to piece together a poem out of On For Time The What And Mister Some Blew If, moving the words around on the white tablecloth, but I couldn't come up with anything that made sense. The two Russians across from me had pieced theirs together and were gesturing and laughing again. I wanted to spill something steaming on them. The first cafeteria poem was read by a short old Russian who wears his silver apartment key, or some silver key, on a shoestring necklace around his neck. He stood up, two tables away from my table, cleared his throat, and read, Trees whine circles in thirsty eve-ninks, my dear only.

It sounded more Russiany than that, but I especially remember eve-ninks, which is evenings, thirsty eve-ninks, and I can understand cold eve-ninks and stormy eve-ninks and windy and happy eve-ninks, but *thirsty* eve-ninks? All the other Russians clapped for the thirsty eve-ninks and I clapped as well only because after the Russian read the poem he bowed to each side of the cafeteria and smiled and sat down. If this didn't entirely seem like a thing a Russian would do who wasn't nice, I asked myself while I clapped, why not? I didn't know and don't know.

The next few cafeteria poems were a lot like the trees whining in thirsty eve-ninks. Snakes rolling teeth and similar jigsawed poems spoken slow and formal like Russians speak. In front of and behind me, at the cafeteria's long picnic tables covered with white tablecloths, the Russians read their poems and clapped for other poems, and I started to panic. I was no closer to having a poem than when I took the words out of the bag, these poor words, and I decided to stand up. Actually, I didn't decide, I just stood up and when I did, decided it was a good idea. I left behind my fruit blintzes and walked toward the exit and before I could open the thick metal door with its square window trapping a grid of strings like tennis racket strings, where you can't see outside until you're right against it, I heard one of the Russians say, Exit Florida Power.

I was starting to feel the quickness from the poem rules and thinking about rules from the made-up games I played with Sally and can't recall, and my poor ziplock of words, then the thirsty eveninks, the Russians clapping, *Exit Florida Power*. By the time I climbed the eight sets of stairs to my apartment, which I do when I remember for exercise, I was, I knew, low. I knew because I went straight to the stove and put on water for hot tea. I had started shivering on the last few stairs, nothing seeming more true than the feeling of being trapped quick inside your body quick inside your body quick inside your body, which is the only way I know to say it.

And five days later—you don't want a sum-up of the five days which . . . the worst thing about low-highness is when you're high and most suitored by the unpredicted joys, you don't want anything to do with them, but when you're low, you beg for the unpredicted joys, and then where are they, you going through the old Tupperware of family photographs again like a punishment, and I can't call Sally because of Steve, alone and lonesome with nothing but time, nothing but time, and where are they?—I finally had my cafeteria poem:

Mister, and if some blew on, for the time what?

I was still low so I went to look for the medicine man.

Indigo Pines and Sally and the medicine man and I are all in Flagler, Florida, named after the man who built hotels a hundred years ago, and railroad bridges across the Keys. You learn this early in school in Florida along with de Soto and de León, who are

Spaniard explorers, and the correct spelling of Florida cities with Indian names like Kissimmee, Sarasota, Palatka, Pensacola, and the Seminoles helping runaway slaves escape from crackers (whites with whips). They don't teach you the railroad bridges aren't there anymore. You have to go see for yourself.

Everyone knows you should bring a gift when you consult a medicine man, so I looked around my apartment for something valuable to me and not him so he can throw it away without regret when I give it to him. I've been to the medicine man about a half-dozen times now, and I'm running out of gifts and the best I could do this time was my only pair of long underwear which you probably don't think you would need in Florida, the Sunshine State, but trust me.

Flagler is Old Florida, which means few tourists. Bel Air Plaza is shaped like an opened-up box with the top off to the left side and the box opened up to the ocean right across Atlantic Avenue. Nobody much shops at Bel Air Plaza, which used to have a magic shop when I was a kid, where you could look at tricks and bins full of fake vomits and fake poos, but now it has a Super Dollar store, Mister Video, and a wig store called An Affair For Hair. Broom is usually behind Super Dollar, which spans the whole bottom of Bel Air Plaza's box shape and faces the beach, so that's where I looked for him, and where I found him, smoking a cigarette on the edge of the loading dock behind Super Dollar, where he works crushing boxes and sweeping. When he saw me approaching with the long underwear, Broom dropped his cigarette and hopped off the loading dock, pivoted the cigarette out, looked at me sideways like people do for effect not real study, and said, Is there a reason you're carrying around a pair of dirty britches, my man?

I saw that he had two oval bright orange stickers stuck to his white Super Dollar apron, one that said *Boneless* and beneath it one that said *Skinless*, like on packages of chicken.

It's a gift for you, I said. The medicine man.

He looked at me sideways a little more. This is just to unnerve you if someone ever tries it on you. The medicine man said, real slowly, A gift. For me. The medicine man. (He laughed, again for effect. Only when I'm low would I know this.) He said, Look, man, I told you: I'm just tan. I live with my grandparents across the street and cain't go anywhere because I cain't drive a car. (*Cain't*, the medicine man said, which means poor and Georgia. Only when I'm low.) He said, I'm no medicine man; I'm no Indian. I'm Dominican, Mexican, Hawaiian, I don't know what. My grandparents won't tell me. I been throwing away all that junk you give me.

We, Broom and I, do this routine every time I come to him. I don't care if he lives with his grandparents, cain't (Georgia) drive a car, and isn't full-on Seminole, which nearly no Seminoles are anymore. I said, I *know* you throw it away. It's what medicine men are supposed to do.

There are plenty of people in Flagler like Broom, people you meet who come off at first as mean and unagreeable but who are mostly, I think, afraid, and probably I'm talking about me, too. Looking for the medicine man doesn't make sense to anyone but me and it doesn't need to, and I've been in Flagler all my life and I don't want to leave. This isn't sad or heroic, really, but I think it's important. Broom wants to drive and cain't, my sister wanted to leave Flagler and cain't. We all have our illusions, I wanted to say to the medicine man, you thought you were telling me something I didn't know. Instead I said, I need some rest.

And as if he had already read my mind, as if he were keyed into my frequency, the medicine man was showing me pills.

Two of these, he said, and you'll sleep like a baby.

I looked at the pills, two liver-colored capsules in a roughened palm, roughened like oak bark or like he'd been messing with car engines. I don't want to sleep like a baby, I said.

The medicine man's hand closed quick on the pills, which he then shoved into the pocket of his light-green Super Dollar slacks, pressed neat with a sharp crease down the side, and I don't think I want to say much more about the medicine man. Think of me, in back of Super Dollar with him and his pills waiting for me to leave like I was at his front door and had handed him a package not addressed to him. I said *thanks* like a question and left, disappointed, like you, maybe.

What's wrong with me? Why aren't I normal? Walking toward Sally's condo from Bel Air Plaza, I watched one of those single-person planes that fly over the beach towing a banner with an

advertisement on it: BOOTHILL TAVERN: YOU'RE BETTER OFF HERE
THAN ACROSS THE STREET, and I frowned because across the street
from the Boothill Tavern is an old cemetery. I frowned even
though I'd seen the advertisement before.

We all have our illusions. When I'm low it's hard to think of anything except how I'm low, anything except me me me, which is like
thinking of the rules to those made-up games instead of the game
itself, being so concerned with how you are doing, or how you are
supposed to be doing, that the *how* overwhelms the *you*, and the
thinking about how I'm low becomes the reason I'm low. But often
enough I find some unpredicted joy that calms me. Pulling over to
let ambulances or police cars pass by, or walking around near the
beach houses, especially mornings before the recycling truck
comes, calms me. Walking to my sister's condo, I noticed a single
blue recycling bin, likely left out too late for the recycling truck,
curbed and open and filled entirely with about two dozen Mama
and Papa Gus whipping cream cartons. Secrets.

By the time I got to Sally's condo, I was feeling sluggish but
anxious, like, have you seen the slowed-down footage of hum-
mingbirds feeding over flowers, with the fastness of the hum-
mingbirds residing in the slowness of the footage? The slower the
footage, the faster the hummingbird feeds. I felt poised for disappointment. I dialed Sally's condo and someone answered and
buzzed me in by pushing seven on the other end of the line. They
didn't even say hello. Sally would've said hello. There's a camera
fixed above the phone in front of the condo which you can watch
if you live at the Admiralty Club, seeing who comes and goes on
channel 32. Steve (Sally would've said hello) must have been
watching channel 32 and answered the phone and pushed seven
on the telephone, which releases the lock on the front door to the
condo, without saying hello, and this probably sounds paranoid,
but it's true.

I walked the twelve flights to Sally's condo, which I do when I
remember for exercise. She lives on the sixth floor, the top floor.
I knocked on the front door with a brass knocker I'd never noticed
before and heard Sally yell, back here. It didn't sound at the front
door like a yell and she meant, I knew, back patio.

I went down the front hallway, through the dining room to the
living room, where the television was turned to channel 32, and I

watched the black and white footage of the phone in front of the condo, where I just was, no one coming or going right now, and the bare light above the phone turned on, which the mailman does when he comes so people in the building can turn to channel 32 to see if their mail has arrived, and I was dreading Steve, whose voice I could hear from where I stood, arguing with Sally about something. He is always arguing with Sally about something.

I know why I don't like Steve, but that doesn't make me feel any better. On the back patio he was saying, Well, let's take it back then.

Sally says, I'm worried. Aren't you supposed to hear something?

Steve: It must be broken. Goddamnit. Where are the batteries? Let's take it back.

Sally: Aren't you worried?

Steve: Of course I'm not worried.

On channel 32 a man has picked up the phone in front of the condo and is dialing, looking at the camera, he must know the camera's there, and smiling and waving, whoever he's calling must be watching channel 32, and he hangs up the phone and goes inside.

Well, Charlie, Steve says. He has opened the patio door, a sliding screen door, and is standing on the track, smiling with his teeth clenched. He says, What you got there?

The underwear. I forgot to give it to Broom and it's been gripped in my hand so long I've forgotten it's there, balled up and useless-feeling, who needs long underwear in Florida, but you do sometimes, trust me, and I say, They were for Broom.

Steve says, I see. The medicine man?

Me: That's him. He isn't official.

Steve: Of course. Listen, Sally's out back, but now's probably not a good time. You understand, I'm sure.

Sally says, Don't listen to him, Charlie, come back here.

Steve walks past me, real close so I have to step forward out of his way so he can pass, and I walk out to the back patio and close the screen door, tossing the underwear behind a potted flower, a white potted flower that looks like an oleander, which are poisonous. Sally is sitting in one of the reclining beach chairs with the white plastic straps and her shirt is pulled high over her stomach, which by now is swelled like a spider stomach and the sight of it, with clear jelly rubbed on her stomach so it shines, surprises me.

Please tell me what you're doing, I say.

She says, Where have you been, Charlie? I've been worried, I've been calling, I left messages with Mr. Sharova. (Mr. Sharova's the superintendent of Indigo Pines.)

I feel terrible, I say. There was poetry in the cafeteria and my words were like on, some, if, blew, what, Jesus. What's that box? What were those games we used to play? When's the baby coming?

Not for a while, she says. Relax, sit down.

I sit in one of the reclining beach chairs, which always makes me feel silly, and look at the ocean for the first time. I had forgotten there was such a pretty view from the back porch of Sally's condo, the sun going down and the sky is peach and clear, the ocean shining, shivering. I look at Sally who's looking at me, and I know I'm going to have a difficult time describing Sally. I've tried and it's like trying to pinpoint why certain smells are pleasing, or colors. She's tan, she wears wire-rimmed glasses, when she's not around she's a sensation I can't separate from the sensing. Here's Steve.

He says, Ginger ale for the mother-to-be, a beer for the uncle-to-be, and a g and t for the father-to-be.

G and t means gin and tonic. I say, I don't want beer. I don't drink beer. (This isn't true.)

Sally says, Do you think we should call the doctor?

Steve: Jesus, no. Calm down, it's Saturday.

Me: What doctor? What's wrong?

Steve: The earphones are broken and now Sally's panicking for no reason. Where'd your underwear go, Charlie?

Sally says something right after this, but I want to tell you the reason Steve keeps asking me about the underwear is not because he cares about the underwear but because he's an asshole.

Sally: I don't feel anything. My stomach's numb.

Steve: The earphones are broken.

Me: What earphones? What's wrong?

Sally pulls out a pair of earphones from the box next to her chair, which look like normal earphones but they're attached by a cord to a white plastic microphone, and says, We're listening for the baby's heartbeat.

Steve says, They're broken.

Sally puts the earphones back into the box and looks at Steve with a sort of relaxed anger I recognize from a long time ago, her looking at our parents that way, but too nice or something to yell at them and him, Steve, like I would, like I want to. Steve. I know he isn't doing anything particularly terrible, just asking about my underwear, which is annoying and not terrible, and saying the earphones are broken, which Sally doesn't seem to think is true, and drinking his g and t (gin and tonic), and saying things like g and t for the father-to-be, annoying not terrible, but trust me.

Sally says, So where have you been?

I say, Mostly in my apartment, going through old pictures.

Though it sounds like all this is happening right now, currently, it, this conversation, the earphones, already happened a few days ago and the reason I'm telling you about it is I feel high right now, and I think what did it was being with Sally on the back patio of her condo. Sally has brown hair which used to be curly and is still curly.

I say, Do you remember any of the games we used to play?

Sally laughs like letting a brief hiss out of a tire and says, Is it the games again, Charlie?

I guess it is, I think but don't say, and I remember I've asked her this before, gone through the old pictures before, but it feels good to ask it, to do it, like going to see the medicine man, and next time I'll probably ask it again. It feels good to have someone to ask questions you need the answers to. It feels good to give Broom a gift knowing he'll throw it away.

Sally says, He used to be such a good artist. (She's talking to Steve but to me really, if that makes sense.) I remember him going to the beach and coming home with like twenty drawings, birds, tourists, dunes. We used to have them hanging all over the house.

Sketches, I say.

They were *good*, Sally says.

Steve clink-clinks the g and t ice cubes in the glass, and I take a sip of the beer I've been holding, which I don't mean to do, but once I do, I take another.

I say, Where'd everybody we used to know go?

Sally says, It's okay.

I want to tell her about the Russians, poetry night, my poor words, Broom, talking to Sally always makes me feel better, not what's said but the saying it, the game not the rules. But there's Steve again, or still, clink-clinking his g and t, too lazy to get another one, maybe, leaning against the patio rail, waiting to stomp out anything I say.

I say, What's it like to have something alive inside you?

This sounds more philosophical than I intend it to, and I'm glad when Sally doesn't answer. Maybe I didn't ask it out loud. Sally wants a family. She used to have long conversations with her stuffed animals, which she collected, inventing personalities for each one of them, and feuds and marriages, and once she walked into the kitchen with a Ziggy doll and held it up to me where I was sitting. I remember the confused expression on Ziggy's face, and Sally said, she was maybe ten years old, she said, Ziggy's dead. Ziggy looked normal enough to me, maybe a little confused like wondering why nothing good ever happens to him, but we dug a hole and buried him anyway and that was that. I hope Sally didn't stay in Flagler to take care of me, but I suspect she did. If so, she married Steve because of me, she's unhappy because of me, my being attached to her is like an anchor being attached to her.

Steve looks like he's going to laugh. He says: So tell us, Charlie, can a medicine man marry you?

A medicine man is allowed to marry whoever he wants, I say, though I don't know if this is true.

Steve says, No, I mean, can a medicine man preside over a wedding, like a priest, or the captain of a cruise ship?

Sally looks at Steve with more relaxed anger, and when someone like Sally is angry at you, you should feel awful, awful. I say, Nothing funny about medicine men, Steve. They *help* people.

Steve says, So do I. He clink-clinks the g and t ice cubes again and I take another sip of beer, and I know why Steve thinks I'm manic depressant. It's because when I'm around Sally, who's the only person I'm not uncomfortable around—when I said before that I used to say I love all people until the Russians, that was a lie, not that I used to say it, I did, but that I meant it, I didn't. When Steve sees me around Sally he thinks I act around Sally like I act all the time, and me hating Steve probably has little to do with him and a lot to do with Sally, whose stomach I've been looking at, the clear jelly shining sort of reddish in the peach light, and it surprises me again, once I realize what I'm looking at. Sally says, Conductant. It's for the sound. She saw me looking.

I say, I would like to listen to the baby's heartbeat.

I don't want to think I said this from meanness, knowing it would make Steve angry, though I might have. After saying it the idea seems like a decent-enough one. I'm the baby's uncle-to-be, why shouldn't I want to listen to its heartbeat?

Steve says, The earphones are broken.

Sally pulls the earphones out of the box again and unwraps the cord because it's tangled around itself and hands me the earphones while Steve repeats, They're broken.

One of the games we used to play involved running around and hiding, but it wasn't hide-and-go-seek. You had to switch hiding places every so often—this was outside at night—in the dark, and you counted to fifty or a hundred and switched hiding places, or yelled when you were yelled at, teasing the person who had to find you. It was called chase something-something. Sally hands me the earphones and I put them on as Steve's talking, saying, Do either of you have a goddamn—

Then they're on, the earphones, no more Steve, and when Sally turns on the machine, which I see says BabyBeat on the side and looks like a plastic microphone, a child's toy, I know right away that Steve's wrong, the earphones are not broken. He's still talking but I'm watching Sally who watches her stomach, the clear shiny reddish jelly, conductant, and I can hear a dead space sound on the earphones like the static sound in between space transmissions, after an astronaut says *over*, that dead watery static sound, and I'm thinking there's something wrong with Sally, something terrible, and she's moving the microphone over the conductant, over her stomach which she's still watching, and I'm watching her, she looks so sad, and Steve's talking *rah-rah-rah-rah*, probably still clink-clinking his g and t, though I can't hear it over the dead space sound, unchanging as she moves the microphone over the conductant, and as I'm getting ready to take off the earphones, which are heavy and tight on my head, Sally moves the microphone under her belly-button, pushed out of its socket, the belly button is, her stomach is so huge, and right before I take off the earphones, I hear a faint *buh-buh-buh-buh-buh*, faster than a normal heartbeat, but definitely a heartbeat, *buh-buh-buh-buh-buh*, fast and faint then louder as Sally slowly moves the microphone higher along her stomach, and I say, Hold it right there.

Sally stops and looks up from her stomach, at me, and Steve stops his *rah-rah-rah*, probably stops clink-clinking his g and t, though I can't hear anything but the *buh-buh-buh-buh-buh*, faster than a normal heartbeat and loud with the dead watery sound beneath it, but now something alive in the water. Sally is looking at me with obvious expectation, holding the microphone on the conductant below her belly button, and there are wide tracks in the conductant from the microphone, and I don't want to say anything because of Steve. I want Sally to know by looking at me. I nod neutrally at Sally and Sally smiles which means she knows and I know and Steve, who is moving toward me to take the earphones, doesn't know, and I'll end here after I tell you what Sally told Steve when he moved toward me to take the earphones and I held the earphones tight to my head, looked at Steve, and Sally said, loud enough for me to hear over the *buh-buh-buh-buh-buh* and the dead watery sound, Sally said, Don't move. I held the earphones tight to my head, already feeling better, and Sally said to Steve, Don't move a single goddamn muscle.

The
Gardener
of
Eden

After his favorite employee died of food poison-
ing, Evan went to the funeral, sat in the back pew, and watched her
husband sob into his open palms while her son followed the pastor's
eulogy with the alertness of someone receiving orders. Tara had
said the boy was in special classes at school, but Evan never found
out if she meant special smart, or special slow. He should have
asked her more questions, he was thinking, he should have expressed an interest. Now, other than ordering the men who worked
at his nursery to take the day off and show up for the funeral—
none had; probably he should have offered to pay them—he didn't
know what to do.

After the service, on the church's back steps, one of the deacons cautioned Evan to eat raw oysters only in months ending in r. The deacon nearly giggled over the simplicity of nature's rules. It was April. Evan watched two pelicans fly raggedly by. The deacon asked Evan what he did for a living. When Evan told him the name of the nursery he owned, the deacon said, "So you do God's work, too." Not exactly, Evan said.

For days after the funeral, he felt disoriented. The newspaper recounted the trial of twin boys in Pensacola who killed their father with an aluminum bat, taking turns hitting him while he napped on a La-Z-Boy. One of the twins, when asked why he did it, said, "He wasn't going to let us go to the game." After they killed their father, the twins indeed went to the game, one dressing up as the high school mascot, the other cheering from the stands. Another article described how the old boardwalk Evan used to fish from had been overtaken by a group of teenage performers who rubbed flammable blue jelly on their chests, lit themselves on fire, and dove off the guardrail into the purling surf. Howlingly senseless, as far as Evan could tell, but people lined up to pay the teenagers five dollars to watch them dive. More and more after Tara's funeral, it seemed everyone was rushing to make bigger noise. Evan felt it himself as well. The funeral left him wanting to do something to mark Tara's passing but he couldn't settle on what.

He met Tidy at the Rotator 5000, an agreeable little bar where Evan could drink beer while slowly spinning in a circle aboard a carousel of stools and listening to Tidy talk about hell. "I can come up with all sorts of things scarier than a burning lake," he said. He wore mirrored wraparound sunglasses and a series of handkerchiefs, two on his head and two rolled and tied around each bicep. "Someone pushing his own empty wheelchair. Metal boots on cars. A woman with pubic hair like a Hitler mustache. *Icicles.* You hear me?"

"I do," Evan said. He was spending most of his evening with Tidy wondering why he was spending most of his evening with Tidy.

The bar completed a rotation every few minutes. Once every go-round Evan had an unimpeded view of a man with a lame left arm shooting pool. Each time the man slunked the arm down on the felt to bridge his shots, Evan winced. He just knew the man was going to implicate the whole bar by doing something embarrassing.

Evan's lack of enthusiasm seemed to stall Tidy's argument. "How was your funeral?" he said, sipping his beer.

Evan shrugged. His view of the man with the lame arm was blocked by a wooden column with a chalkboard on which someone had written *Weak Schedule Gators*. A song about cheeseburgers played on the jukebox. Evan grew impatient. He knew Tidy was too drunk to unload his dissatisfaction on. "Poorly attended," he said.

Tidy finished his beer and motioned to the bartender in the center of the carousel for another. "Never again will I eat at the Porpoise," he said.

The man with the lame arm took a pack of cigarettes from his shirt pocket, freed one, lit it, and returned the pack to his pocket. "I sent the husband and son five thousand dollars in an envelope," Evan said. "Had it delivered to their house just after she died."

Tidy nodded vigorously, rocking in his stool almost. "That was the correct thing to do, Evan. Generous, instinctive, I'll bet you didn't even think about it, just *did* it. When I look around—" He looked left and right. The carousel seemed to have picked up speed. "I see a lot of idle . . . *idling*. No one's disposed to grace anymore, no one's even pointed in that direction."

"I've got plenty of money."

"All I see are ghosts, scarecrows, feminine bother!" Tidy yelled this loud enough to be heard over the part of the song where the singer listed all the things he liked on his cheeseburger. The female bartender pushed the tap closed midway through Tidy's beer and stared at him. Tidy said, "I'm talking about myself too. Come on, keep pouring. I'm just saying that my friend here's a major donor, a deeply generous man!"

"Quit that," Evan said, and, to the bartender, "Not true."

A little while later, Tidy paid his tab with two rolls of quarters, crossed his arms on the bar, laid his head on top of them, and closed his eyes.

"Getting off," Evan said, and the bartender flipped a switch beneath the beer taps that stopped the rotating bar. Evan hopped off the carousel and nearly fell.

When he got home he sat on his back patio drinking grapefruit juice that tasted like the can it came in. His house sat on the

Donna River, one of many brackish intracoastals that made mile-wide peninsulas up and down the eastern coast. Today the water was low and calm enough for egrets to hop from glimmering oyster bed to glimmering oyster bed, ardently nipping at the smiling shells. Daylight had begun to dissolve to dusk, Evan's favorite part of the day. He could hear the sound of airhorns miles south, two honks for the drawbridge to open, four once the sailboats they were attached to had passed through. There was something narcotic about being surrounded by so much water. It came as an urge, a feeling of ceaseless migration which, in his twenties, he had thought was lustfulness, or immaturity, but which he had long accepted as life.

He listened to his phone ring, a few thoughts clacking around in his head like nickels in a lunchbox. He focused all his concentration on listening to it until it stopped. Egrets continued to step over the oyster beds, pecking at the shells. The entire existence of the oyster was devoted to squeezing its valves tight enough to keep its shell shut. Evan remembered a billboard he had seen a few days ago, advertising Bob Barry's Bail Bonds. Above a tanned girl in a pink bikini and handcuffs on her wrists, it said, *I Came to Florida On Vacation . . . I Left On Probation.*

Untrue! Turn it around, though, and you had something. You come struggling to take life seriously and you leave on a bucket of bad oysters. *Oysters*, even the name was ridiculous. Egrets were ridiculous, stalking around the oyster beds with their backward-bending legs and gangly dignity. Evan was tired of everything being ridiculous.

He'd bought the Garden of Eden nursery from a Pentecostal named Joe Tull when it was a small seasonal outfit. Though Tull had stopped by the nursery every week to change the proverb on the sign out front, he only opened from October through December, to sell customized Christmas trees. Tull assured Evan that if he changed the name or the "mission" of the nursery, the specifics of which Evan was still hazy on, it would fail. "Trust me on this one," Tull had said. "I have it on the *highest* authority," with the assuredness of a man gambling with someone else's money.

Tara was hardworking and serious, a part-timer with a degree in dendrology and a stern gracefulness that struck Evan as recently attained. The last time he saw her he'd driven her home from the nursery in the work van. She lived in a tin-roofed carriage house on an overgrown plot outside of town. Evan navigated the van down the dirt-rutted drive. As he neared the house, the growth slackened and gave way to chinaberry shrubs and fruit trees, beautifully maintained, bordered with neat rows of date palms and live oaks and, sitting by itself near the edge of the brush, a dapple-trunked tree, of a kind Evan recognized but whose name he couldn't immediately summon.

But as he got out of the van and moved closer to the tree, which was small and sprawling with pointed oval leaves and green crabapples not yet ripe, he remembered. Manchineel. The telltale sign was the trunk, mottled white from the tree's caustic sap. Evan stood next to it, studying the trunk. As a kid, he and his father had come across a few manchineels, down in Cudjoe Key as the two were canoeing through the mangroves. His father pointed out the tree to Evan and, for the rest of the afternoon, listed all the ways Caloosa Indians had used it. They mashed the crabapples to make poisonous stews. They worshipped it. They danced around it naked. They tipped their arrows with the sap and killed Ponce de León.

"I haven't seen one of these in years," Evan said. "I thought the state cut them all down in the seventies."

"My husband says our son's gonna try to climb it one day and kill himself. But I don't have the heart to remove it. It seems determined to live. The old woman who sold us the house said she kept it here to remind her that good and bad aren't inherent, in nature or anywhere else. She was a bit crazy. She wrote letters to notable women asking if they could send her one of their fake eyelashes. She had nearly a hundred of them."

Evan studied the tree and listened, resisting the urge to run his hand over it. The crabapples looked like blanched plums. "What does it remind you of?" he asked her.

"That I don't have the heart to remove it."

Looking at the manchineel, he remembered his father drinking gin from a plastic cup in the canoe, calling the Caloosa Indians *Noles* like the college mascot. Evan rubbed his hand over the bark, lightly.

"Careful," Tara said. "I've seen blackbirds die from less."

"If you ever decide to have it removed," he said, withdrawing his hand, "you should let me know. I wouldn't mind grappling with something poisonous."

"Sort of biblical work?" Tara said. "Sounds like your sort of job."

Evan watched a lizard scuttle up the trunk of the tree, stop, and then scuttle back down. "The nursery's not religious anymore," he said. "It's religious *themed*."

Tara smiled at this. The wrinkles around her eyes relaxed Evan, as if they showed that her reaction was well-worn, normal. "Like Disney World," she said, holding the smile for a few seconds, shaking her head. "I wondered why we sell shot glasses."

"Things may have gotten out of hand. I guess we're misleading people."

Tara dismissed this with a wave. "I wouldn't worry too much about it," she said. "When people quit grasping, *then* it's time to start worrying."

Wind blew through the manchineel and its spiny leaves held on and twitched. Insects hummed, palm fronds rumbled. Under the overcast sky, the gleaming silver of the carriage house's tin roof had changed to a drabber gray, and Evan could see cloudy spots of bird droppings the color of sumac berries. He began to speak, then hesitated on a sudden feeling of consequence. It was one of those moments when all seemed in flux and he felt like he could proclaim anything, anything.

But he had never been the spontaneous sort, and he wasn't sure where to land now. "It's lonely," he thought to say, and this was close, but not close enough. His longing came clumsy and untenable. He said, almost to himself, "Looks like rain."

"Shoot." Tara was holding her right palm upward. Evan had felt the drops too, but didn't connect them with the fact that they were standing directly under the manchineel. One landed on his arm and immediately left a red welt, another stung the base of his neck. "We should get out from under this thing," she said.

He didn't move. He was waiting for her to finish consoling him, though he'd never felt particularly guilty about the nursery and wasn't sure if he did now. Here before him was an adult, someone who regarded the world seriously enough to dismiss some of it for him. More raindrops fell on his neck and head; the water felt superheated. Tara patted him on the shoulder and said, "Be glad," and walked away. Standing in the rain, Evan watched Tara retreat, the muddy rings around the legs of her jeans. Had she felt it too? Thinking about her, welcoming the sting of the burning leafwater, Evan waited as she went inside the house. She waved from the screen door, he left.

He'd appreciated her presence at the nursery. They didn't talk much, and when they did, their conversations were mostly impersonal and work related. He wasn't aroused by her; when he drove home after a busy morning, he seldom continued to think about her, and when he did, the thoughts were general, vague, benign. There was no hesitancy or anxiety, no meaningful declarations unspoken, no poking around for signs of marital disharmony. Only the afternoon under the tree in her yard, three, four minutes of his life. And the phrase, "Bad oysters are being blamed," the last sentence of the article about her food poisoning.

He sent Tara's husband and son five thousand dollars, a sum that seemed both meaningless and sort of vulgarly generous. He'd waited behind the church, after the deacon walked off, for them to leave. He wanted to say something to them, respectful yet unequivocal, brief yet expansive. He'd rehearsed a few to himself: "She was a joy to be around." This was inexact. "I'm very sorry for your loss." He was miles away from an adequate gesture. The funeral-goers got into their cars and withdrew from the parking lot until all that was left was Evan's MG, a rip in the vinyl top that flapped in the wind like a blown sail, and Tara's husband's Volvo. When he and the son came out, Evan flicked his cigarette into the grass and offered a few sympathetic words while the father nodded.

"We should be going," he said. "Thank you for coming."

Evan extended his hand. The father looked at it for a moment then shook it. "If you need someone to cut down that manchineel," Evan said. "I'd be happy to."

"Excuse me?" He put his hands in his slacks and jangled his keys. Though they had met once before, he didn't seem to recognize Evan.

"The tree, the poisonous tree in your front yard."

"You must be from the nursery."

The boy was staring dreamily at the pearl buttons on Evan's shirt. Up close, Evan could see that Tara had meant special slow. His pale skin reflected the parking lot's sodium vapor lamps, which had just buzzed on, and he had the sort of fancy silken blond hair you see on toddlers and lingerie models. "I know you," the boy said, looking up from the buttons. "How much do you think she'll weigh in the tubes?"

"I'm not sure," Evan said.

"How much will she weigh. I know what I think."

"Thank you for the offer," the father said. "We need to go home now."

"You really should have it removed," Evan said. "Manchineels, they're dangerous. It wouldn't take my boys more than an afternoon."

"I need to know what you think," the son said.

"That's very generous of you," the husband said.

"I mean it," Evan said.

"Something to think about. Thanks."

It's the least I can do, Evan began to say, but the father and son were retreating to their car. The father held the boy's hand, and the boy looked back every few steps to smile at Evan. Evan followed them, pulled the roof back on his car, and watched the Volvo drive away. Listening to his engine sputter and flood as he tried to start it, he was thinking: the least I can do is also the most I can do. *My boys.* How insubstantial. He pumped the gas pedal twice and counted to sixty.

At the nursery, the newest thing was Prayer Cactuses. Evan's customers were going crazy for the potted cholla and prickly pear he bought cheap from a guy in Jacksonville. The cactuses were part of the man's drug operation; Evan wasn't clear exactly how. The idea was, you prayed over the Prayer Cactus and the prayer came true.

Loay, Evan's Sudanese delivery driver who equated anything resembling criminal activity with deportation/four years' military service/certain death, was wary of "the cactus man," as he called him, so this week Evan had to drive an hour and a half to and from Jacksonville. Tara had made the trips when she was alive, returning late in the afternoon and unloading the cumbersome plastic sheaves herself. Evan disliked handling the destitute flora, but the markup on the cactuses, certainly stolen, was huge, plus they were easy to maintain, so north to Jacksonville he went.

On A1A, Evan read the signs. There were several messages from God, black billboards with "Do you know where you're going?" and "Where have you been lately?" on them. Questions attributed to God personally, designed to attack confidence. The motels, many of which had just reopened for the season, had "American Owned" and "Clean Towels" on their signs. One sign said, "Scream, kids! They'll stop." On either side of the road were parallel "You Are Now Entering" signs. Evan entered Wilbur-by-the-Sea, Ormond-by-the-Sea, Marineland, Crescent Beach.

Wind blew sand and plastic grocery bags across the road. Every so often, an oncoming car would flash its high beams at Evan indicating a speed trap ahead, and Evan would slow down. At times an exchange like this might strike him as joyful or hallowed, but today he paid no attention. He was thinking about the night, years ago, when he had uprooted a few dozen sea oat clumps for a developer building a hotel inland, an offense punishable by five years in prison. He wondered if he was capable of leading a scrupulous life. On the floorboard near his left foot were two crushed Diet Rite cans, which he knew were Tara's. He opened the van door at a gas station in Palm Coast and kicked the cans onto the asphalt.

When Evan arrived at the cactus man's house, he was watching a parade on television. There was a colored assortment of glass bongs on the coffee table in front of him, perfectly lined up, one after the other, like organ pipes. "The Gardener of Eden!" he said when Evan had identified himself and walked into the house. The living room smelled like heating oil and cat piss. "Where's Eve?" he said, which was what he called Tara. "I been looking forward to a visit from the agriculture princess all day. Straightened up." He pointed to the bongs. "Even took a bath." The cactus man, shaved head, faint acne scars, abiding smirk inside a goatee, looked just as he always did. On television a group of children on a parade float were dressed up like the fifties.

"She died two weeks ago," Evan said.

The cactus man, whose name Evan did not know, let out a hoarse laugh. Apparently he thought Evan was joking. "You ever been to a naked beach, Evan, a *nude* beach?"

Evan, standing next to the cactus man, watched him watch the parade. His eyes radiated vapid wonder, each new image on television revealing something unexpected and terrific. The cactus man stared straight ahead, mouth ajar, uninterested, it seemed, in standing up. Evan hated the way druggies imposed their stunted tempo on everyone around them. "The fuck are we doing?" he said suddenly.

"Nothing, really," the cactus man said. "Damn. I guess I'm kind of trying to figure out what this parade's a*bout.*"

"Why don't we get on with it then."

The cactus man sighed. "I was expecting you to be Tara. Tara has a much more harmonious demeanor."

Outside, Evan loaded the plastic trays into the back of the van while the cactus man watched. It was clear that at some point in their transport the cactuses had been skillfully grafted and prepotted. The chollas, fist-sized and packed in sandy soil, were intricately entombed by crisscrossing white barbs. A plastic stake next to the bulb said *The Prayer Cactus High-Quality Prayer Tool. It Works!* Other than that they were, as far as Evan could tell, normal cactuses. When Evan finished loading them, he paid the cactus man, sulking with his foot on the van's back bumper, two hundred and fifty dollars. The money cheered him up instantly. He said, "Hey, need anything else before you go? A bong hit? Guns? *Dude,* I got some baby crucifix saguaros coming in from Nogales next Tuesday." He extended both arms to demonstrate the shape. "In full fucking bloom!"

The cactus man looked so cheerful and certain with his arms out. Evan told him he'd call with next week's order. He closed the back door and got into the front seat of the van. After Evan had started the van, the cactus man walked around and said through the open window, "Hey, tell Tara I said . . . you know."

"No," Evan said, "I don't know."

The cactus man smiled. "Sure you do."

"No," he said, "I don't."

"Catch you on the flipside. Tell her I said that."

When Evan returned, Loay was working on the sign in front of the nursery. It didn't matter that, of Loay's many responsibilities at Garden of Eden, it was possibly the least essential. He was not the type to favor one duty over another, though clearly he took great pride in maintaining a conversation with the motorists on Peninsula Drive. He operated with the clarity of purpose of someone who has worked hard to understand a new language and, finding it less difficult than expected, is eager to reach a level of mastery beyond those around him. Evan allowed him to change the sign whenever inspiration struck. Loay had already taken down yesterday's message—*Remember people the prettier the flower the more careful the care. All praises due*—and was putting up a new one. It read, so far, *Don't be afraid.*

Done with the day's invoices, he watched Loay from the window. Loay was attaching another letter to the suction cup on the end of the extension pole and bringing it up to the sign, sliding it into its slot. With the letter in place, he stepped back to make sure it was properly aligned. He worked with extreme consideration, a deliberateness that Evan thought was distinctly African, but maybe not. Loay was the only African he knew. Three hours ago he'd asked Loay to deliver a pair of dwarf palms to a house in Lakebridge, a new subdivision. "I will make it my duty," Loay had said. The dwarf palms were still leaning against the chain-link fence on the back lot, their roots packed in sand and burlap. Another letter up, slowly, slowly, into its slot. Loay again stood back to evaluate his work. Seeing Evan standing in front of the window, he waved and smiled.

Don't be afraid to mulch your empty spaces. All praises due.

Evan sat behind the counter and read a book about poisonous trees. He planned on enlisting Loay and driving to Tara's house after work, and offering to cut down the tree. "It is a dangerous job," the book said, about removing manchineels. "When the chainsaw bites into the tree, squirting sap can blister skin and even blind you if it gets into your eyes. Burning the tree is no better—the sap is carried in the smoke."

A teenage girl who smelled heavily of bath products walked into the store, looked around, and seeing Evan at the register, said, "This place have any holy oil?"

"Holy soil?"

She pulled a wrinkled piece of paper out of her pocket and read, "*Oil. Anointed oil.*"

Evan directed her to the Christian Superstore near the interstate. When she left, the little bells on the front door jingled.

Loay, finished with the sign, put the tools away and came into the store. "Have you had time to reflect on today's message?" he asked Evan.

"It's beautiful, Loay. Maybe it'll sell some mulch."

"Ah, you are too close to the messenger to see his message," Loay said. He sniffed the air. "And it is so *stagnant* in here. It smells like dead rosebuds."

Evan pressed *No Sale* on the cash register and took out a stack of credit card receipts, which he stapled together and put in a basket beneath the counter. Loay was still sniffing. His hair stood out in short, orderly dreadlocks, balled at the ends like chess pawns. Finished with the receipts, Evan said, "Didn't see you at Tara's funeral."

"Ah, that is because I didn't *go* to Tara's funeral." He reached behind his back and carefully untied his apron. "I spent the afternoon poolside at my apartment complex. I had intended to go, but while cleaning myself I realized that I have been to far too many funerals, and far too few swimming pools."

Loay lazily pulled the apron over his head, mindful, Evan was sure, of his own baffling slowness. Evan felt like grabbing the apron and tearing it up. "You've landed in the right place," he said. "Everyone seems to have arrived at that conclusion with you."

"I remember something Tara once said while we were clipping Easter Ferns. She said, 'If Evan were any better he wouldn't be as good.'"

Evan flinched. Though he couldn't help thinking it sounded like something Loay had made up, he felt a pull of melancholy appreciation, out of proportion to the moment. He stared at a stain on the floor and waited for the moment to pass.

"And now she is dead," Loay said. His thick eyelashes fluttered and he smiled a placid smile. "It's very unfortunate. What else can be said?"

"Plenty. I don't know. More."

"What?"

"I said I don't know."

"See? That is why poolside is better."

Loay nodded with his eyes closed and rubbed at the stray hairs on the base of his chin. "Here is a story," he said. Loay always began his stories by closing his eyes and saying, "Here is a story." "In my first English school, several years ago, we were given a book to read about a captain aboard his ship which has been damaged and is taking on much water. The captain's crew ties him to his helm to die alone, and they leave in a lifeboat. The ocean takes so long filling this ship, it allows the captain to consider all that he is regretting, from his adult life back to his child life. He is ankle-deep in one chapter, waist-deep, shoulder-deep in the next. Just as he figures out what he regrets most, surprise!, the captain is rescued.

"In class the next day, the teacher asks me, 'Loay, please tell us what the ocean symbolizes in this book you've just read.' I think, *symbolizes*? I offer the first answer that plops into my head. I say, 'Water.' A few classmates laugh at me. The teacher says, 'No, Loay, what I mean is, what does the ocean *represent*?' Ah, now I think, *represent*. This word means equally nothing to me. I let the word marinate in my mind. After a minute or two, aha!, I got it. Yes, it is a trick question, you see. I say, '*Salt*water.'"

Loay smiled and his shoulders arched forward slowly and slightly like a leaf closing. He was pleased with himself. Most of the time Evan welcomed his stories—they made the slowness of the afternoon more tolerable—but after thinking about Tara, the idle anecdote stung like a spur. He should have been able to muster at least some fake reverence once in a while. "Can't you tell when someone's being serious?" Evan said.

"There is nothing more serious than my story."

Evan wasn't listening anymore. He locked the cash register, put the keys in the pocket of his jeans, and hopped off the stool. "I need you to help me with something."

Loay slumped his head and checked his wristwatch, big, black, and cheap. "You want me to deliver those baby trees before I go home?"

"I've got a more important job for you."

"First, please, will this job involve me fraternizing with felons or cactus men?"

"No. I just need a good man to help with a tree removal."

The bells on the front door jingled. Before Evan could turn around and say, "We're closed," Loay said, "Aha!" He clapped his hands together and smiled. "And who better to fit that description?"

Evan turned around to see Tidy wearing sunglasses, the usual two handkerchiefs on his head, and a tattered maroon athletic outfit. He looked like a wrestler from an impoverished country. "My dogs!" he said, taking off the sunglasses. "I've come to mulch my empty spaces."

Loay bowed and retreated.

―――――

"Is the African religious?" Tidy asked in the van. He was tapping both hands on the glove compartment, using his right heel on the floorboard for a bass drum. "He looks religious. I mean, he looks like the *founder* of a religion. Those messages on your signs? That hair? Shit. Are your employees required to take any kind of oaths?"

"My employees aren't required to do anything."

"He makes me jittery," Tidy continued. "You know the movie where the witch doctor blows a palmful of blue dust into Martin Sheen's eyes, knocks him dead *out*, buries him alive? Every time I see the African, I think: uh-oh, here comes the dust. The African has a despot's phrenology."

Tidy said this whenever Loay was brought up. Sometimes Evan tried to remember exactly how he befriended Tidy. It seemed to him that Tidy just walked into the nursery one day, as he did today, and announced that they were friends. The more Evan knew about Tidy, the less Evan understood him. He cut lawns. He swore it was the most pointless thing a man could do for a living and that he wouldn't consider doing anything else. He had a mechanical engineering degree and the word *Jam* tattooed on his upper arm. Evan had never seen his hair. He kept his head covered with bandannas, claiming he didn't want anyone examining his skull. Evan was pretty sure Tidy had no hair.

Driving toward Tara's, Evan felt good. There was a calmness that came between departure and arrival, a feeling he had always been aware of, but today it seemed particularly authentic. He felt like telling Tidy that they were driving to Tara's house because he, Evan, had decided to mark her death properly, because she deserved something more consequential than a funeral. And maybe this was the reason. But he couldn't deny that a part of him wanted to cut down the tree so he could stop thinking about her, that removing the tree was a door-closing gesture, for him, not her.

Tidy was still drumming on the glove compartment. "It makes sense to worship the moon," he said, and nodded toward the horizon, where the moon was huge and near full in the afternoon sky, hazy as an apparition. "The perfect god: go days and days without thinking about it, and there it is. The closest heavenly thing."

Evan steered the van down the long dirt-rutted drive. When the dry brush gave way to the clearing where Tara's house sat, Evan noticed a neat row of cars in front of the house, expensive European sedans with bumper stickers supporting various causes. Also: the manchineel was gone. He parked and walked to where the tree had been. It was now a scorched patch of ground with wavering lines of turned-over earth. Someone had burned it down. Evan stood over the scorch mark for a few minutes and studied it, surprised only at how unsurprised he was to see it gone. He was annoyed as well, with the husband, with himself, but mostly at the fact that the lone possible response to Tara's death—and seeing the empty space where the tree had stood proved this was so—had been carried out for him, without him. Burned it. Probably killed every bird and bug within a thousand yards. He ran the toe of his boot over the black stumps of grass.

On the way back to the van, he noticed a piece of cardboard staked into the ground. Shaped like a headstone, the sign said:

R.I.P.
I was no match
for Dr. Danny's Tree Undertakers.

Evan uprooted it, brought it to the van, and tossed it into the back.

"Where is this?" Tidy asked.

"Tara's house."

Tidy nodded solemnly, as if this was all he needed to hear. "Never again will I eat at the Porpoise," he said.

Evan felt like honking the van's horn, so he did, four times. It made him feel better. "You know something, Tidy," he said. Tidy nodded again. Evan looked at his own reflection in Tidy's sunglasses, his face fisheyed, all pleading and nose and unshaven jowls. He could hear the faint rise-and-fall of screams coming from the woods beyond the house, the sound of collective laughter. A party. "Neither will I," he said.

Evan got out of the van. "Come if you're coming."

As the two walked toward the house, the noises became louder. Now, accompanying the screams and laughter, was frenetic, drum-heavy music, a song that went, "Joy . . . and pain is like sunshine . . . and rain."

Evan led Tidy past a woodshed, a gas grill, and a furrowed plot with weathered beanpoles leaning at dismaying angles. In the backyard, shaded by slash pines, were a group of about twenty children jumping up and down, hemmed inside a huge canvas-walled square pit, which appeared to be filled to the top with soap foam. Some of the children wore helmets, and even before Evan could get a good look at any of them, he knew by the howls and the crab-wobbly way they moved, that they were, like Tara's son, special slow. All fanatically paddled around in the soap, scooping it with their hands and tossing it in front of them. The bubbles would hang briefly and then fall.

"America," Tidy said.

Evan and Tidy stopped at the corner of the house, under a roof awning and out of view from the children and their parents. The adults stood a few yards from the pit, sipping white wine while their children frolicked. Not all the children were retarded. They were jumbled around, some alone, some in groups. Evan watched a big black-haired boy with Down syndrome run toward a girl and tackle her into the bubbles. A few seconds later the girl surfaced, laughing and looking slightly guilty. Tara's son jumping up and down by himself in a corner. He was paddling the bubbles with both hands and looking utterly overwhelmed by what had overtaken his backyard.

After awhile the parents took off their shoes and joined the children. They danced awkwardly at first, holding their wine glasses carefully in front of them with both hands, but as the music picked up they began to move a little wilder. A few were jitterbugging, some disco-danced. A man in a bow tie and black vest stood outside the pit with a wine bottle wrapped in a napkin, waiting for the parents to come by and refill their glasses.

Tidy began taking off his boots.

"What are you doing?" Evan asked.

"Into the foam, man. Into the foam."

Evan made no attempt to stop him. Tidy ran toward the pit, hopped over the canvas wall, and began doing jumping jacks in the bubbles. The song that was playing now went, "I wanna know, I gotta know, I feel like knowin.'" Apparently, neither the parents nor the children were fazed by Tidy's intrusion. Evan could tell that they, the parents, had very little in common with one another, except their disabled children. That this had brought them all together struck him just then as joyous and perverse.

Currently, Tidy was jumping up and down with his arms raised in the air like a disturbed pelican. Some of the kids were following behind him, trying to imitate his dance. He yelled to Evan. "Get in here. This stuff is all right." He said it *ah-ight*. Tara's husband was dancing too, or doing a modest imitation of someone dancing. He looked fairly devastated. There were deep bags under his eyes, which stared wistfully at the gas grill. Evan figured this party had been planned for a long time, and the father thought he should go ahead with it, keep his chin up, hope for the best, and so on.

Evan took off his boots and laid them next to Tidy's. He walked slowly to the pit, carefully stepping over the wall, and then stood waist-deep in the bubbles. He expected there to be water underneath, some sort of resistance to wade through, but the bubbles were like nothing. He tried to dance a little, but felt foolish, so he walked around in a circle behind the children who were following Tidy. On his second time around the pit, Evan broke off and walked over to Tara's son, who was still by himself, paddling in the corner. He wore glasses with bits of foam on the lenses. Evan stood in front of the boy and bobbed up and down. The boy smiled. "Pro*fes*sional," he said. "Wasn't this *good!*"

"The bubbles," Evan said.

"Good!" the boy insisted. "I saw you." His top teeth were pristine and his face as free of expression as a squirrel's.

"Okay," Evan said. The boy made him uncomfortable, but he continued to bob in front of him. The song went, "Bow-bow nuh-uh no no no." Every once in a while the boy would scoop up a handful of bubbles and throw it at Evan.

"I saw you," the boy repeated. "In the rain. Mommy didn't want me climbing the tree. She tried to let it stay and now it isn't. But *she's* gone with it."

Evan's shoulders tensed. The boy stared at him intently, eager to be fully comprehended. Evan couldn't help himself. "Where's your mommy now?"

The boy brought his arm out of the bubbles and tapped his finger on his forehead. "The tubes," he said.

"Poor dude doesn't even know his mom's dead," Tidy said as he danced past. "Doesn't even know enough to be sad about it."

"Wasn't this *good!*" the boy said, glaring at Tidy. Evan could see tiny dim veins on his half-closed eyelids.

The parents had joined in behind the children, and everyone was doing the conga from corner to corner. Somebody grabbed Evan and he became the leader for a few minutes as they danced past the man with the bow tie, who kept the bottle of wine tilted. Another person handed Evan a full glass of wine and he drank it. On the next go-round, the man with the bow tie refilled Evan's glass. He could feel the awkwardness diminishing, the trick that the first drink of the day played on him. Tara was dead, but look at all these bubbles. Evan could imagine the boy in the window, watching his mother standing below the tree she told him not to go near, curious about who she was talking to and why. Evan wondered when he had become the sort of person who got attached to things only after they were gone. The song quickened. After another glass of wine, he decided it wouldn't be a bad idea to begin hopping, and when he turned around, everyone behind him was hopping as well. The song went, "Loo loo, la la, loo la loo." And Tara was still dead.

Evan broke off from the line and returned to the boy, who held his finger to his forehead. The boy said, "Under the tree. In the rain. Did you see *me?*"

"No." In the boy's buttonhole, Evan noticed, was a single dandelion, tied around and knotted by its fibrous stem. "But that doesn't mean you weren't there."

The boy hooted at this. Tidy danced by and said, "Poor little dude."

The foam receded. Some of it had dissolved, some of it had been tossed out of the pit. Evan watched the father dancing alone in the corner. Every so often someone would lay a hand on his shoulder— listening to them speak, the father nodded solemnly, wearing a look of perpetual reluctance. Evan could feel the silence that would be waiting tonight for father and son once the guests drove away and the two of them returned to the house. An impossible silence, it would be the sound of the absence of sound. But for now, in the foam pit, the music was playing and everybody danced. And another song played, and then another.

Ursa,
on Zoo
Property
and Off

At Thursday's committee meeting my coworkers and I decided that the animals at the downtown zoo had been locked up long enough. It was starting to weigh on us, we moved, so we passed a motion that it was time one of them was liberated, and passed a counter-motion to do something about it, and a second counter-motion to do something about it right away.

But how best to choose an animal to free, Mosedale wondered aloud, one on which our labors would be fully warranted? Which prompted some discussion.

"Tired as it is, I'm a fan of the bald eagle," said someone near the back of the room. "Imagine unlatching a metal gate and watching a bald eagle fly upward, upward toward autonomy?"

"Isn't it endangered or something?" Robison asked.

"I've never even seen a bald eagle, except TV ones," Mosedale said. "Glenn and I went to the state park, which was supposed to have them. That is one beautiful American creature, I'd say. That's a turkey vulture, Glenn would say. There's one again! I'd say. Turkey vulture, Glenn would say."

We decided the bald eagle wouldn't do.

"Hey, what about dolphins?" I said. "Dolphins are highly intelligent, highly evolved."

"If you ask me, sea life is too damned cocky," Mosedale said. "Ashaming as it is, I've always felt intimidated by the dolphin. It doesn't particularly *need* me for anything I can see. The dolphin seems a little *above it all,* if you catch my drift."

We moved to charter a bus to the zoo and see for ourselves which animal we most wanted to liberate. If we were patient and lucky, one of them would step forward and announce its worthiness. The appropriate animal would make itself apparent, we were sure.

With that settled, we carried on to other, less revelatory deliberations. Stevenson, for instance, kept noticing dampness on the employee kitchen carpet. His shoes made a squishing sound whenever he waited for his pot pie to finish microwaving. Mosedale, for one, suspected leakage.

A few months ago I decided to stop shaving, which I'd always disliked but had never before thought to not do. I had been shaving for nearly fifteen years, skipping a day only when I was too sick to get out of bed, until one morning in the bathroom, razor poised, I resolved not to do it anymore.

The beard grew in thinly and unevenly at first, and was auburn-colored in places, dark brown in others. Sometimes at the bathroom mirror I'd be convinced that the beard made me look prophetic and vital, and other times, shabby and ridiculous. I would swing from one appraisal to the other, never settling in between.

In the small office where I worked, the beard caused much excitement. My coworkers began calling me Moses, or Trotsky, and winked and smiled knowingly when I walked past their desks. They pretended they were only having a little fun with me (ease up, Moses!), that their teasing was good-natured, and I played along, receiving the comments the same passionless way you'd regard something loud and mostly harmless. A stuttering moped, say.

I had actually intended on shaving the beard after a few weeks, but the more my coworkers teased me, the less inclined I was to shave it. And the longer the beard grew, the less my coworkers disguised their displeasure with it. Soon they began leaving anonymous drawings and notes on my desk.

One of my favorites: *What is it you are trying to prove? It's no wonder you can't find a woman. The sight of you makes me angry.*

(This was from Hodges. I recognized her handwriting.)

I threw away the drawings and notes, resigned myself to receiving more, and carried on with my job, carried on with my beard-growing.

On the way to the zoo, aboard the tour bus, everybody sang rousing songs. Sterne, an émigré from Albania, or Armenia, claimed to know more than 4,000 folk songs. He would sing a verse in his native language, which his wife would translate and which we would then repeat. Some stood up to sing, others sang in their seats. I sang in my seat. I enjoyed being looked at by the other motorists on the highway, even if the windows of the bus were darkly tinted and my face mostly hidden. It was their lack of resistance I enjoyed, the naked one-way envy of the thing . . .

We sang another song, which went: And how is your health? So what! And how are your children? So what! And whose problems are these? So what!

My coworkers had brought their children and husbands and wives along, and the bus had an eager, rowdy aspect to it. What would happen? What would we see? In the seat next to me Carter from the mailroom was talking on a cell phone. A sallow twenty-two year old with urban tendencies, he wore a shiny fitness suit and his thin blond hair was plaited into cornrows.

"She's toe up, man," he was saying. "At first I thought she looked all right, but then I thought to myself: nope, this girl's totally toe up."

He went on like this for a few minutes, describing exactly how this girl had fooled him into thinking she wasn't toe up, and how after a few days with her he began to suspect her of being toe up, and how he finally had to admit to himself that yes, she is absolutely, irretrievably, toe up. Noticing me listening, he turned to me, put his hand over the tiny phone's receiver, and said, "You mind?"

At the zoo, we moved off in different directions, onward, leftward, ahead, on. We had a lot of ground to cover. Untract the strollers! Secure the toddlers! Everyone worried especially about the toddlers: were we right to bring them? Already the toddlers looked confused, their faces swollen with hesitation, as if to say: how will we be expected to remember our time here?

The zoo's sidewalks were a geometry of day-glo animal tracks that directed visitors to corresponding exhibits. Bear tracks to the bear exhibit, elephant tracks to the elephants, and so on. I followed a set of green monkey footprints, looking down at the tracks while I stepped over them. They weaved and veered off here and reconverged there, and seemed to forecast some perfect future exodus.

The tracks ended at the door to the lesser-monkey exhibit, which was a converted greenhouse filled with tethered oak stumps and lesser monkeys. Macaques, specifically, a dark, intense-looking monkey found in Indonesia, and zoos. From the front the macaques looked normal enough, tromping around inside the greenhouse, chasing one another with sticks. Some of them tapped anxiously on the glass when they noticed us standing there. A promising sign! I waved and smiled, careful not to show my teeth, and one of them waved back, bouncing on its stubby legs. I decided it liked my beard. Two more macaques approached the glass, one old and ragged, the other brand-new looking.

Noticing the tumult, more zoogoers approached the exhibit, and a few more macaques walked up to the glass, and everyone was waving and tapping and smiling. Someone snapped a picture, and the macaques jumped back, spooked by the flash probably, and scurried away from the glass. When they turned around, they revealed these grafted, pink ass-helmets, jagged and dire looking. It was a sight I was completely unprepared for. The things stretched like exit wounds from the small of the monkeys' backs halfway down the rear of their thighs, heart-shaped, vascular, a vital and separate part of the animal.

Looking around at everyone else, I saw that I wasn't the only one taken aback. Many lingered there open-mouthed in front of the glass. Crowell's son, who pointed and snickered, was the only one able to respond to it.

And then one of the macaques stumbled to the edge of its pen, turned around, dangled its hind end over a concrete ravine that separated it from us, and casually crapped into the abyss. For at least three minutes it did this, clutching a low oak branch and yawning. The second I was positive he was finished, out would come another.

A zoo volunteer in a "Friend of the Earth" baseball cap made her way to the center of the crowd.

"All right," she said. "Looks like everyone's noticing the macaque's swollen rear haunches."

We nodded.

"Aren't they magnificent, aren't they simply majestic?"

Myers began circling the group with his right hand over his eyes, blindly pawing at the air with the other hand. There was a palpable sigh by those acquainted with him. Myers, it was well-known, had a fondness for the dramatic. Once Myers got started there was really no stopping him.

"Unsubtle god!" he said. "Blind me now or signal that you approve of this tainted scene!"

"You might ask why some of them are more swollen than the others," the volunteer continued, undaunted. "See that female over there, the one whose haunches have a sort of glistening-pink rosy hue?"

Myers started convulsing and bumping into other zoo visitors. He wore shorts and had these skinny hairless thighs that pulsed taut as he pantomimed, saying, "I'm spoiled! I'm spoiled!"

"Come off it, viceroy," a woman behind me said.

"The nastiness is burned forever on the cinema of my soul! Jukebox of misery! I'm spoiled!"

"Somebody smother him with something," Morris said.

"The haunches make absolute sense, biologically," the volunteer said. "Think of the haunches as nature's odd calendar, or if you prefer . . ."

I took leave of the lesser-monkey exhibit before the volunteer could explain the biological reason for the macaque's swollen haunches. Biological reasons were necessary but they weren't always sufficient. For now I preferred the swollen haunches to remain a mystery.

The more I walked through the zoo, the more I realized there was no discernible logic to how the animal exhibits were arranged. Willful disorder: this was the type of thing that would always bother me. Camels next to lizards next to tortoises next to sea lions. Similar geography? Similar life habits? Random, random, random. The camels chewed with these broken-oyster-shell teeth and seemed to beg to be handled unfondly. The giant tortoise hung glumly on.

In its pen a sloth bear paced automatically back and forth, taking eight nearly identical steps every time. When it neared the end of its run, it raised its paw with a flourish, turned, and went back the other way. It made me think of a prison inmate, which made me again think of my coworkers.

The truth was I'd never really liked my job to begin with, and my coworkers were the main reason. Early on, even before the beard, I'd never really hit it off with them. All of the women in the office were quiet and attractive and hopelessly married. The men were smug and proprietary. They interrupted one another, laughed at their own jokes, prefaced comments with, *If you ask me*, perspired a lot, and were balding or bald. They fouled up my office, which was next to the employee kitchen, with the smell of their microwave pot pies. Every day, I'd have three or four clumsy interactions with them. For instance, Collins came into my office the other day and said that he'd seen me riding my bike downtown. He yelled my name but I was too far away for me to hear him.

"Thank you," I told him. "Thanks." He didn't know what to make of this so he left.

Everyone responded the same way to my beard, which by now had gotten, I'll admit, slightly out of hand. For starters, it was impossible to keep clean—food and dirt and what-all got caught in it—and it shed everywhere. I would find coarse red hairs on my desk and in my food. I was a bit disgusted by it, and I imagined they were too, but I had also grown fond of it.

There at the sloth bear exhibit, I absently ran my fingers through it, along my jawline and the meaty tendons of my neck. The main reason I hadn't shaved was because I thought it would be cowardly to conform so easily to office opinion. Lately, though, my face had begun to itch, and I considered getting rid of the beard. I wasn't sure how to do it. Quietly and unceremoniously? Cutting the beard a little each day, drawing out the process? In a month or two, I'd be clean-shaven again, and hardly anyone would notice. No, that wouldn't do. Often lack of ceremony was what was needed; the difficulty was knowing exactly when.

Next to me a man was saying that the reason the sloth bear paced so ardently was that he needed to "investigate his boundaries," a normal and instinctive animal behavior, he said, for sloth bears. I breathed easier, reassured by the official sound of the explanation. Who of us didn't investigate his boundaries on occasion? Who was I to argue with instinct?

Next came the beavers, who were impressive. How could you not admire the beavers' assiduousness, the way their bodies had evolved into their work? Using their tail paddles, they constructed a dam above a modest basin of water, swimming from dam to shore adding to the mound of downed branches. Four struggling beavers, each busy on a different task. A cold-water smell filled the air by their exhibit, difficult to describe. I stood on the bottom railing and watched the beavers' progress. I envied the one whose job it was to sit on the shore and gnaw branches, patiently testing the branch with his paw every so often. It was the type of activity you could watch for a long time and think nothing at all. Or maybe just: there they go again.

They never had it so easy as they did here at the zoo: they apparently didn't recognize their confinement at all. They worked hard and ate well, unbothered by predators. In the morning, zookeepers probably disassembled the dams the beavers had constructed, and the beavers would rebuild them again.

Though it had always seemed a little wanton, I nonetheless esteemed—if that is in fact the appropriate word for it and I don't think it is—the beaver. If I had thought the beavers would enjoy the manmade lakes of suburbia more than the streams of captivity, I would have freed them right then, on the spot.

———————

At noon, my coworkers and I met for lunch at the outdoor lounge, a collection of zebra-, tiger-, and leopard-patterned plastic tables and chairs. Something on the menu called a Giant Panda Burger caught my eye, but the description of it said it was just a normal hamburger. As incongruous as it seemed to be serving meat at a zoo, there it was.

My coworkers chatted with one another with an air of disappointment. As far as I could tell, the animals were not brought up.

A waitress in a dark-brown bear suit took our orders. The suit had mustard and ketchup stains on the legs, and gouts of fur missing. Someone asked if it got hot inside there in the summertime and the waitress—Ursa, the nametag read, probably a zoo joke—Ursa said, yes, yes, it did. The words echoed inside the suit and made her sound boyish and far off and lewd. I was instantly, irrevocably attracted to her. Of course you were, you're saying. Of course I was. The voice was not so much lewd, I decided, as naively suggestive. I imagined her a reckless employee and figured I would compromise myself in her presence and then spend months coming up with ways for her to forgive me.

Telephone operators, call-in radio voices—it was always the women I could hear but not see. Seeing Ursa, I wondered which was more gratifying: a human in an animal suit or an animal in a human suit?

Did they even make human suits?

(On cue, at the table next to mine Harris did an impression of a prairie dog coming up from its hole.)

How about a human suit filled entirely with water moccasins?

The moccasins could writhe around and swim, head to toe, allowing the suit to move, waving to other human suits as it walked to work. Imagine: an entire office of water moccasins in human suits! I thought of my coworkers moving automatically through their days, delivering and receiving, answering the telephone, nodding, gesturing, posturing, floundering.

But what would be most gratifying, what would be most wonderful, would be to step forward with a knife and cut the suits from navel to neck and stand back while all the moccasins spilled out. That would be something I'd like to witness.

Ursa in her bear suit came back and set a plateful of food in front me, ketchup, steak sauce, salt and pepper, some paper napkins. "What type of bear are you?" I asked her.

"I don't know. Brown, maybe. No one's discussed it with me."

The eyes of the suit were orange painted glass, while Ursa's stared out of the bear's flared nostrils and looked lost: dim, tentative tunnels. They were pretty.

"Hey, let's suppose I came across your type of bear in the woods. Would I be better off running the opposite way or remaining very, very still?"

Not her eyes themselves, I mean, but how her darkened brow tucked in and out as she listened and did (or didn't) understand. Her eyes looked lost only because of the movement around them.

"They caught me stealing boxes," she said. "Wearing the suit's a punishment to them."

"Stealing? Boxes of what?"

"Just boxes. Cardboard boxes. Big ones."

Because you couldn't tell much from the actual eyes. Alone, they were dim or watery or hazel, but they weren't confessional, they didn't reveal or change at all with the conversation. Even the bear's bright orange marbles looked natural enough, considering, and were similarly expressive—that is, not at all—as Ursa's own just then.

"I see," I told her. Which was almost entirely false.

"All the suits are discipline problems." She motioned over my shoulder toward a trio of animal suits—giraffe, zebra, ostrich—who were, I swear to you, doing landscaping next to the reptile house. The ostrich weed whacked a tall chinaberry shrub, while the zebra swept the felled clippings into a giant-sized trash bag.

The giraffe stood by and surveyed the others' work, a lit cigarette dangling from its fat yellow neck.

"What a wonderful," I started to say to Ursa, but Ursa had gone.

I unfolded my napkin and bit into the Giant Panda Burger, which I disappointedly remembered was just normal hamburger, and coughed. I wiped the crumbs out of my beard, combing through it and inspecting the napkin until it came up clean.

Ursa walked out again bearing a plate of steaming red chicken wings for Harris. The crotch of her bear suit sagged despairingly to her knees. I chewed and watched an empty popcorn cone tumble by, tumble by in the wind.

After lunch I went into the restaurant's bathroom: low paneled ceilings and gray lockers along the wall. A bumper sticker on one of the top lockers said *I'm a Caring Consumer!* I soaped off my hands and inspected myself in the water-spotted mirror. Nothing in my beard, some flecks of black pepper in my teeth. Eyes, normal. Tongue, dry, singed-looking. I noticed an overnight bag sitting on the row of lockers behind me.

While I was here, I could trim a little hair from my chin, maybe, or lose the moustache. The idea of shaving my beard in a zoo restaurant bathroom seemed peculiarly apt. A deal: if I found a razor in the overnight bag, I'd shave. If I didn't, I'd let it keep growing.

In the bag was foot spray, aspirin, toenail clippers, a split-open Pall Mall, hairpins, matches, and a travel-sized tube of ladies' shaving cream and package of blue disposable razors. I popped the cap off the shaving cream, lathered my neck, freed the clear plastic safety guard from the razor, and, guiding the razor under my chin and tearing at the tangled hair, cut myself. I rinsed the razor under hot water and tapped it against the yellowish basin. Another pass along my chin, another gash. A warbling, minor, gratifying sting. The bathroom air thickened with steam and menthol, the mirror fogged up. I worked slowly, throwing away the razor after fifteen or so passes with it and opening a new one. The more I gouged and nicked myself, the more intent I became on not leaving the bathroom until I was totally clean-shaven.

Nearly halfway through, with only two razors left, I tried the toenail clippers, which actually worked well on the longer hairs, and didn't cut me too badly as long as I was careful. I wiped the mirror clean as I worked, briefly surprised each time by what I saw.

"Homo sapien!" I said to the mirror when I was finished.

Ignoring the dozen still-bleeding nicks on my face and the space above my top lip, which looked to be about four inches wide, and also my nose, more scalene than I'd remembered, it was certainly an improvement. I stared at myself, temporarily unfamiliar, until eyes, nose, mouth, chin gradually cohered, biasing my appraisal. I splashed water on my face and wiped the remaining shaving cream from my neck.

Walking toward the Great Ape House, I felt the wet, warm air on my naked jaw. I wanted to make a declaration to the zoo's transient human and permanent animal citizenry. It was one of those moments when every quivering thing is exposed and positively intelligible, and you wish you had a more honest vocabulary with which to answer it.

At the entrance of the Ape House was a sign reading, "Gorilla Think Tank: It's Not What You Think." Inside, behind glass, a mother gorilla nursed her baby. Her back was turned to the glass and she peeked over her shoulder every once in a while to see if her audience had cleared out, shifting herself from view. The chattering mass of people outside her window clearly worried her. She peeked and shifted again while the baby gorilla's raisiny hands gently kneaded at its mother's side.

"*Hey*," Mosedale said. "Look at us!"

The gorilla started to grow impatient, adjusting more vigorously to obscure herself from our view. We grew impatient, too. No one would say so, but all of us badly wanted to watch her watch us watch her. At least I did.

"My god, she thinks she's modest!" Morris said. "It's nothing we haven't seen before." And then, noticing me for the first time, "My man, you are wounded."

I dabbed at my neck with the bottom of my shirt. "Don't mind me," I said. "Go back to what you were doing."

"If you ask me," Hodges said, "you should have kept on with it. Just the other day Meadows and I were discussing how nearly through we were harassing you about it."

"Look like Grizzly's gone executive!" said Carter the mailroom attendant, who had just walked in. And, noticing the mother gorilla: "*Damn*, monkey titties!"

"The beard gave you a lowdown and hazardous quality," Mosedale said. "Now you look just like the kid brother on 'You're Too Much, Uncle Sammy.'"

Everyone laughed, including Mosedale. Unfortunately I was familiar with the character Mosedale was referring to. He was this short, kind of bulb-headed kid who, in the episode I watched, had tried to persuade Uncle Sammy to buy an ice cream truck.

Behind the glass, the mother gorilla shifted again, concealing herself from view. Her refusal to turn around for us was delicate and willful. It was difficult not to accept it.

In a separate room, a group of orangutans sat around a large wooden spool. Spread out on a floor of dry hay, they touched their hands to their chests and noses. They looked to be communicating to one another in sign language.

Another zoo volunteer, another "Friend of the Earth" baseball cap. She had the generally rough and guileless demeanor of people who work closely with animals. Around her neck was a black plastic whistle on a shoelace.

"These males have learned to sign," the volunteer said. "Taters, the one in front, can recognize some 6,000 words. He scores about the same as a four-year-old child on language tests."

Hearing this, Taters stood up and signed to the volunteer, who signed back.

"And then what?" someone asked.

"What do you mean?"

"What do they get for that?"

"By teaching them to describe their time here, we're discovering that humans aren't the only ones who are capable of complex communication."

"What do they say?" I asked. "Do they ask to be set free?"

I saw from the volunteer's expression that this was a foolish, an unnecessary question.

Connors said: "I bet they make fun of everyone looking at them."

Hodges: "If you ask me, they probably just talk about how sick and tired they are of one another. In there like that all day. I can't imagine. How long do they live?"

"A long time!" Connors said. "Bring on some *female* orangutans, they're saying!"

"Actually," the volunteer said. "Right now Taters is saying: *man, face, blood, unfortunately* —"

"Hey, how come those monkeys aren't wearing any pants?" Hodges's daughter interrupted. Everyone paused for a moment to laugh and applaud the little girl's ingenuity.

I too was momentarily distracted by the comment. Looking down at the constellation of blood marks on my shirt, at my pants (tan, wrinkled), and at my shoes (vague, cheap), the whole notion of clothing seemed preposterous to me.

I remembered the story about the British scientists who, having seen for the first time a colony of wild gorillas and capturing them, had tried their luck with some of the caged female gorillas on the return voyage. And had failed in violent and varied ways—in fact, some had died trying. How long did it take for the scientists' awe to turn into proprietorship, proprietorship into wanting to screw? Those who survived claimed the female gorillas had somehow hypnotized them and seduced them through the bars. The scientists were rumored to have worn makeshift gorilla suits to fool the monkeys, a detail too absurd to not be true.

Leaving the think tank, I remembered why I stopped going to zoos. Always the same comments by fellow spectators about the animals acting worried, sad, happy, mad, curious, tentative—*just like us!* I didn't agree at all. They weren't anything like us. This wasn't because of the obvious physical differences or intelligence or evolutionary differences. It was the careless way we conceived of them. We needed to begin considering them not according to what they could learn or imitate or be taught, but to what we ourselves could not.

I made my way toward the zoo's exit and looked for other people who were by themselves, but couldn't find any. Young couples and babies, babies, a lot of babies. In rented strollers and dual-sided carriages, on foot, attached to nylon safety-leashes. I was struck by a swell of hazy lassitude. My cuts had begun to dry. As I drew near a man wearing sandwich boards advertising the Shoe Barn, he handed me a flier that said *Everything Must Go.* I stopped in front of him and waited for the knowing wink, the portentous smile. He nodded to me and said, "Move along, champion."

Although *Everything Must Go* was an excellent slogan, at a zoo, at a zoo especially, I was hesitant to make much of signs so obvious. I sat on a planter near the exit and waited for the bus to pull up. I was done with the animals. I'd never really intended on freeing one or, more likely, now that it looked hopeless, I convinced myself I had never intended to. Next to me a pair of sunburnt women sat down and began a disagreement about mosquito candles. The sun was going down.

After awhile, I went back to the outdoor lounge to look for Ursa. The animal-print chairs and tables had been cleared out and gathered into a pile, strung together with metal cable, and locked to a birch tree. Ursa stood at a makeshift bar and sorted silverware into a four-compartment tub, struggling to grip the forks and spoons with her gloved hands. I told her that I'd like her to come home with me.

She dropped the last handful of silverware into the tub. "Why not," she said. "Let me go clock out and get my things."

I caught myself looking into the bear's bright orange eyes again for a flicker, a signal. Nothing.

"That's it?" I said. "Why not?"

"What did you expect?"

"I expected: sorry, no. Or just: no."

"Well: sorry, yes."

"Thank you," I said. "No, I mean, good."

It occurred to me just then that Ursa might not recognize me. I considered asking her whether or not she did, but I thought the question might damage whatever understanding we had.

"How will I know you when you come back out?" I asked her.

"You won't," she said. "You'll have to take my word for it."

I imagined her smiling inside the suit, kind of half smiling to one side.

When she went inside, I looked for a place to sit down and, seeing none, stood. Plastic bags hung in pine branches, blowing around like, blowing back and forth like—like what? I didn't know. As the last traces of daylight dissolved, walkway lamps winked on and on. The painted animal tracks glowed and wavered under yellow blooms of light. I felt good.

When Ursa came out again, she was still wearing the bear suit. I sighed, relieved.

"My manager reminded me that I'm required to stay in costume while on zoo property."

"That's okay," I said.

Out of habit, probably, she waved to children as we walked along the path. Some waved back and some looked genuinely frightened, perhaps unable to reckon this bear with the one they had just seen pacing in its quarters.

"Everybody responds to you," I said. "You're a kind of minor celebrity."

"Tomorrow's my last day. In the suit."

On the tour bus my coworkers looked displaced, physically stunned. I thought Ursa's presence might strike them as a fitting, even extraordinary, conclusion to our day at the zoo, but no one said a word about it: in fact, everyone seemed to have totally forgotten about our initial reason for going.

"Nothing was free there," Walker kept saying. And then, realizing she was being misleadingly oblique: "Even the free maps, I mean, cost fifty cents."

"I saw a sculpture of a sloth brain," Hodges said. "I saw buzzards hopping with their wings clipped."

The bus thundered down the road. Nobody talking, just the broad low hum of the motor. After a while Crowell, sitting in front of me, turned around in his seat and pointed. "Hey, look over here, everybody! Delilah's cut his beard! Check out Delilah with his face full of nicks!"

"Samson was the one who had the hair," Myers corrected him. "Delilah cut it off."

"He's Samson *and* Delilah! He's victim and perpetrator both!"

"You're too much, Uncle Sammy!"

Minor cackling. I didn't care, though, really. Across the aisle from Ursa and me, Stevenson laughed and shrugged stupidly. His wife caught me staring and sort of apologized to me with her eyes. That is, with her eyebrows.

Ursa brushed off the legs of the suit with both paws, her bear head lazily tilting forward. The suit gave off a dirty, sweet smell, like old grease.

"Have you seen the beavers?" I asked her.

"The ones down by the lesser monkeys?"

I nodded and, realizing she couldn't see to the side of her, said, "Yes."

"Sure I've seen them, but those don't belong to the zoo. That stream is outside zoo property."

"Who do they belong to?"

"Themselves, I guess. I don't know. No one."

"They're their own beavers."

"What's that?"

"I said I'm glad."

"I can't hear anything inside this suit. I should probably take it off now. Your coworkers look like they're beginning to summarize me."

"No, no. Don't take it off just yet," I said. "Let them summarize. They live to summarize."

The driver turned on the interior lights, making it impossible to see anything outside the bus except the glare of passing headlights. I knew the other drivers on the road could see inside the bus, though, and I gazed out the window, coveting their view. In a way, I dreaded the moment when Ursa would finally have to take off the bear suit. Women were equipped with a sensibility I had always labeled longing, or dissatisfaction, but which I had begun to suspect might be exactly the opposite of that. What I mean is, they seemed to reflect, without ever accepting, whatever longing or dissatisfaction was aimed at them.

The bus rumbled on and Ursa and I waited quietly for what would come and the émigré, awake now, surveyed the two of us. He began singing what sounded like a mournful song. His wife translated: Listen to me, and I'll tell you the story of a man who made his home inside a bear's den.

Listen to me, he sang, and I promise no lies . . .

The
Volunteer's
Friend

Tate is at the hospital again, watching a wall-mounted television screen, following the camera as it worms its way around the bright pink walls of his lower digestive tract. It moves quickly, forward and back, stopping on a patch of tissue for a second or two, and then off again. The nurses warned him that the camera's progress would feel like bubbles rising and bursting in his abdomen, and indeed it does. On television his colon looks slick, enormous, almost inhabitable. He closes his eyes.

The last time he was here was with his wife, Jeanne, two years ago. The antiseptic smell of an examining room is a smell he now associates with her, the velcro rip of the blood pressure cuff. He can hardly stand it. But the pain in his stomach has become too insistent, the symptoms too certain, to ignore. He's waited long enough to know that waiting won't fix what's wrong with him.

"There," the doctor says.

Tate opens his eyes. "What?"

"A lump, a discoloration." A tiny white plus sign appears on the television, followed by another a few inches lower, and then a third and a fourth. Four straight lines connect them and form a rectangle. Within the rectangle, Tate sees a bulging scuff mark the color of a cheap tattoo. "Right there," the doctor says. "It could be nothing. Could be more than nothing."

———————

More trips to the hospital, more tests. The doctor uses terms familiar to Tate from his wife's illness: biopsy, colonoscopy. He drinks two gallons of liquid that tastes like charred grapes. One final test, and the nurse is making a joke about the weather. She tells him he should get dressed, which he does, slowly, before going to the doctor's office to wait. Through the office's curtainless window is a wooden jungle gym with a chain bridge where a young girl sits, head down, legs dangling between the slats. The doctor walks in and closes the door. Spiky-haired and young with purplish eyelids, he looks like one of those television prodigies. Tate steadies himself. The lump, the discoloration are more than nothing.

"There are several courses available to the patient," the doctor says, then corrects himself. "To you."

The worry is it spreading to his liver or his lymph nodes which, the doctor explains, pointing to his own neck, are important to his immune system. Tate wishes someone had come along to listen to the doctor for him, as he did for Jeanne. How he clung to each word then, searching for the smallest possibility of hope! He doesn't have the energy to go through it again. He turns back to the window and the girl, whose neck, Tate sees, is covered with livid burns. The girl stands up and jumps into wet sand, wet from a heavy downpour earlier; in the examining room, the nurse said, "Thought I might have to come to work in a rowboat."

Currently, Tate realizes that the doctor is attempting to comfort him, and that he should say something. "I wish Jeanne was here," he says.

"Understandable." The doctor probably saw Jeanne's name somewhere in his paperwork. "I could have someone from the hospital come by your house. To talk to you. I could do that."

"No, no," Tate says. "I'll be all right. I shouldn't have said that out loud."

The doctor is scribbling something in his notepad.

A few weeks of treatment and Tate feels raw and worn out. He's been fitted with a permanent catheter in his chest which makes it difficult to sleep. When he does sleep, he dreams he is contagious and has to walk around in a surgical mask, handing out cards explaining his illness. The only foods he eats regularly are bananas and toast. All else leaves him nauseous or planted on the toilet for a half-hour, or both. He brings catalogs into the bathroom and reads through them, clothing catalogs, catalogs advertising imported and hard-to-find candles. When he stands up, there are warped red marks on his thighs from where he's rested his elbows.

He receives get well cards from the same people who sent sympathy cards two years before. One of the cards depicts a glass of wine and says, *A little aging, a certain amount of mellowing . . .*

Not long after she was diagnosed, Jeanne decided to redecorate the condo. She'd read an article saying there were two types of living spaces: *healing* spaces and *weakening* spaces. She wanted a healing space. Slowly she started getting rid of their things and refurnishing the condo in an Oriental style, searching through flea markets and junk stores for anything fitting this description. Whenever Tate tried to talk about her sickness, Jeanne changed the subject or ignored him. She didn't want to discuss being sick or getting better, she wanted to talk about the perfect new tea table, or the limited-edition Confucius figurines.

She never did get a chance to finish. Much of their old dark oak furniture remains, but now with jade plants and bamboo window shades, watercolors of flute-playing courtesans on the walls, pillows stitched with Chinese characters. A month after the funeral, a wooden abacus arrived in the mail, which Tate hung in the kitchen above the toaster oven. Now, waiting for his toast to finish, he studies the abacus, two beads in one column, five in the other. It's one of those things that gives no hint at all as to how it works. In the kitchen, in the condo, Jeanne is everywhere visible, nowhere present. Sometimes, Tate feels like putting an ad in the paper, selling it furnished, and moving.

One afternoon, after a leucovorin treatment, after the doctor has asked how he feels, Tate admits that he wouldn't mind having somebody visit. "Understandable," the doctor says. This is his favorite word. A few days later, a volunteer from the hospital stops by. She wears cumbersome sunglasses which she removes when Tate answers the door. She is young with far apart blue eyes. Her name is Callie, she tells him, short for Calandra.

"Very nice," she says in the foyer, stepping out of her sandals. "Very eclectic."

They sit across from each other in the living room. He offers her a glass of water; she accepts and insists on getting it herself. Her silver anklet makes a tiny sound when she walks away. Tate reaches down to the floor, picks up a paperclip, and pockets it. He has no idea what to say to her. When she returns she drinks the water in a single long sip. Finished, she reaches into her purse and pulls out a book called *The Big Questions* which, she says, she always uses when meeting with new friends. By *friends*, Tate understands, she means the people she volunteers to visit for the hospital. "Are you ready?" she asks, opening the book.

He assumes she'll offer something vague and impersonal. Instead she asks, "Would you be willing to tear the wings off a rare and beautiful butterfly for an all-expense-paid trip to anywhere in the world?"

He thinks about it for a second, then says, "Do you mean right now? Right this minute?"

"Right now." She crosses her legs, skinny with a tan line just above the anklet. "I hand you a rare and beautiful butterfly and all you have to do is tear its wings off for a trip to Paris."

"I've already been to Paris. Years ago with my wife, Jeanne. She was born there. Paris was about what I expected it would be."

"You can go anywhere, Tate. Africa, China. All you have to is—" She makes a tearing gesture with the book.

"I've never been to China. I guess I'd pick China."

"So your answer's yes?"

He tries to think about the question, but keeps stumbling on the opposing condition. What does killing a butterfly have to do with traveling? The girl is straightening the corner of the page, which has been dog-eared, looking at the page with raised eyebrows, distracted but aware of his hesitancy. "Of course not," he says. "I've never enjoyed traveling alone. Plus the butterfly. No, my answer's no."

"There's no correct answer," she says.

"I don't like that one. Try another."

The others are similarly baffling. "Your wife and child are bitten by a snake and you only have enough antivenom for one of them. What do you do?" The questions are intended to be thought-provoking, but mostly they confuse and depress him. The girl stays for a little over an hour. When she leaves, Tate washes her glass and sets it on the drying rack. From his kitchen window, he watches her get into a small black car, sit for a few minutes in the driver's seat, and then drive off.

He's glad the hospital sent a woman, though he wishes she were older. His neighbors are nosy; if they see her leaving his condo, they'll assume something lurid is going on. Jeanne was always cordial to them, and they think this means that Tate will be too. They'll ask, "Do you have some family visiting or something, Tate?" hoping to surprise him into an admission. He isn't interested in befriending his neighbors and sees no reason to pretend otherwise, especially now. If one of them asks, Tate decides he'll say no, his family isn't visiting. His neighbors are free to assume what they want to assume.

Callie visits twice a week. Tate learns that she went to college to study nursing, but never finished. Now she wants to be a writer, or maybe a film director. Currently, she says, she is happy volunteering at the hospital. She sees no reason to go back to college to study writing. "I want to be able to draw from a variety of experiences," she says. "I already know what school's like." She talks about herself as if from a great distance looking back. Once in a while she stammers over a word—"I enjoy spending time with seer, se-ries"—pauses, closes her eyes, and then begins the sentence again: "I enjoy spending time with serious people." She means him.

They walk to a park a few blocks from his condo. The park was once a little petting zoo with dwarf goats and alpacas where Tate used to bring his nieces and nephews when they came to town. That was a long time ago. Now, young couples sit together read-ing the newspaper on bedsheets in the overgrown grass. Some boys throw a frisbee. It lands in front of Tate, who hands it to Cal-lie, who tosses it back to the teenagers. The two sit on a metal pic-nic table so Tate can catch his breath. The sun is a blinding smear shape, so intense that Tate, in a floppy hat that Callie insisted he wear, feels its individual rays all around him. Callie wears sun-glasses, her hair pulled into two thin braids. Tate looks around for a bathroom while Callie describes the plot of a book he's never heard of. He's had to pee since they left the condo but is too em-barrassed to tell her.

A middle-aged man in oil-cloth coveralls approaches, smiling with his mouth open. "I know a woman haunts me all night long," he sings. "I know a woman with a body won't quit—"

"Go away, Adam," she interrupts.

The man regards Tate. His shiny lips seem poised on an insult.

"It's a song," Callie says after the man walks off. "And the cov-eralls, they're just ornamental. Adam doesn't do anything all day but creep people out and loiter." She exhales loudly and then looks at him. "Are you okay, Tate? Are you hot?"

"I'm a little warm. We should probably go back."

But when he stands, his insides constrict, and he knows he won't make it to the condo without finding a bathroom. He looks around again and says, "I really need to use a bathroom. Soon."

Callie smiles slightly before catching herself. She lifts her sun-glasses and looks around the park, at him. "Well, I believe we have no choice but to find you a nice large shrub."

She leads him to the far end of the park. The boys stop their Frisbee throwing to watch her go. They look as if they want an explanation. Behind a red-budded hedge that separates the park from a row of aluminum-sided duplexes, Tate unzips his pants and Callie stands watch over the park. He waits. He breathes deeply, tries to relax, waits some more, but nothing happens.

"I don't hear anything," she says. "Tate? Are you having stage fright?"

She walks behind him and he fumbles with his pants, struggles to zip them up. "This is extremely common," she says. "Listen, you need to straighten your back, relax, and breathe."

"Would you go stand where you were?" he says. "I don't need any help with this."

"Deep breaths," she says, backing up. "Know that I'm not the sort of person who's passing judgment." She begins whistling chaotically and Tate straightens his back and relaxes. Cloud wisps blow past the sun, dimming the ground behind the hedges for brief intervals. He closes his eyes and shivers.

On the way home, Callie says things like, "It's extremely common," and, "Don't think a thing of it."

He doesn't want to talk about it anymore. "The man from earlier," he says after awhile. "How do you know him?"

"Adam? He's someone I used to visit for the hospital," she says. "He was sick."

"What happened?"

"He got better." She crosses her arms, then leans forward to wipe her mouth on her hands. "Often I have that effect on people."

Tate can't tell whether or not she's joking. This would be a good time to pay her a compliment or to thank her for visiting, but he can't think of a casual enough way to say it. He doesn't want to scare her. Arms crossed, a half step in front of him, she looks lost in thought. They walk back to the condo without talking.

Slowly Tate's appetite returns. Though he's still worn out, especially on the days he goes to the hospital for treatment, the nausea starts to subside enough for him to eat at the Scripp's again. When he returns from the hospital, he lies down and almost instantly sinks into a black sleep. Waking up, his eyes coming into focus on the muted watercolor of a panda bear, it takes him a second or two to figure out where he is. He puts on a nice shirt and drives to the Scripp's, a restaurant he and Jeanne went to for forty years. Often the waiters, many of them as old as Tate, leave a second menu and place setting across from him, out of habit.

The last time he and Jeanne ate there, Jeanne, while finishing her salmon, bit into a staple, which she spat out and gave to him. Tate showed it to the waiter who returned with the chef. "I'm very sorry," the chef said. He was fat with a neat beard. Tate expected Jeanne to shrug him off. "I want you to go into the kitchen and bring me a piece of red-velvet cake," she said.

The chef turned to the waiter. "We don't have red-velvet cake," the waiter said. "We'd be happy to bring you anything from our dessert menu."

Jeanne looked at Tate and sighed and smiled. "I want you," she repeated, "to bring me a piece of red-velvet cake."

The waiter and the chef returned to the kitchen. Tate finished his dinner, ordered more wine, and waited for Jeanne to make a move to leave. Probably they didn't talk about anything while they waited. Often they didn't. After twenty minutes, the waiter returned with a three-tiered slice of red-velvet cake with white frosting. Setting it in front of Jeanne, he said, "Please accept the restaurant's apologies."

She stared at it for a second, then asked the waiter to put it in a box for her to take home. The waiter left with the cake. "What am I doing," she said.

At the Scripp's, Tate waits for his dinner while reading the newspaper. The waiters quietly move from table to table, talking to diners who look as if they've been herded up and taken somewhere against their will. An unopened menu sits across from him. Sometimes Jeanne would order her dinner, then realize she had chosen the wrong thing and go search for the waiter. Though it annoyed him then, he misses those few silent seconds after she handed the waiter the menu, when she'd either stand up or smile contentedly at him. He misses the anticipation and release of it.

Tonight, Tate orders the lamb chop and a glass of red wine. He drops his fork, then reaches over the table for the extra one. Though he never said it to Jeanne, he always assumed she'd be the one left alone after he died. Driving around town, reordering her days, making arrangements.

Callie begins visiting his condo three, sometimes four times a week. Her water glass from the previous visit is still in the sink when she returns. On the days she stops by, Tate makes sure not to wear shorts, because his chalky knees look sepulchral. Or cardigans: they make him look too brittle and kindly. He uses the bathroom before she arrives and pulls a comb through his thinning, colorless hair. He imagines Jeanne watching and disapproving of these preparations, and he feels slightly foolish. But he isn't interested in examining his intentions. Being with Callie is too easy. He feels a vague air of aspiration whenever she comes over.

A man from the hospital calls one morning to ask how the volunteer is working out. Tate tells him he has no complaints. "None at all?" the man asks.

"Nope," Tate says.

"Would you like to think it over for a second?"

"Would you like me to have a complaint?"

The man lets out a brief wheeze. "Sir, this is a courtesy call to ensure our volunteers are adequately performing their duties."

At first Callie reminded Tate of Jeanne when Jeanne was younger, but he realized that this was a false impression, invented perhaps to make him more comfortable around Callie. Jeanne at twenty-four was steady, forthright, aggressively unmysterious. Her only wile was the French accent, which diminished slightly over the years—or maybe it hadn't diminished; maybe he'd become accustomed to it. Sometimes he has the feeling that neither of them changed at all, they just became blindly accustomed to each other, satisfied with what they knew and what they didn't. And that Jeanne, even now, especially now, is as intimate and invisible as his nose.

One day Callie reads him a story, about a ship full of soldiers returning home from battle. In the beginning, two soldiers are talking about a third, who has tuberculosis. She reads so beautifully clear and unwavering that he is soon too distracted from the story to figure out what is leading to what. At the end, one of the soldiers is wrapped in a sail cloth and dumped off the stern of the boat into the sea. Sharks circle him and take quick teasing bites. "I'm so dumb," she says when she closes the book. Her expression is grave, consoling, almost convincing. "I just remembered it being an amazing story, especially the end. I didn't even think about the subject matter."

Tate hasn't either. "It was lovely," he says.

"You seem so calm," she says. "I'm speaking from experience. You don't act like anything's wrong."

"I've always been calm," he says. "And I've been feeling better. The treatment seems to be working."

She nods. "Everyone agrees it's an excellent hospital." She's still grave, though, the expression not yet ready to expire. "The reason I always wanted to go into nursing was because at hospitals something, you know, *vital* is always happening. I spend hours in the lobby of the oncology ward talking to patients. It probably sounds terrible."

"I don't like hospitals. My wife, Jeanne," he begins, then, seeing Callie brighten, stops himself. Something about the sudden lift of her eyebrows. "She didn't like them either."

"You're so unsentimental. My other friends are always wanting to confess things to me. I guess it's a side effect from their medication. Not that I mind. I like it actually. You, though, have an even temperament. Probably you should've been a judge, or an airline pilot."

What sort of things do her other friends confess to her? he wonders. Sometimes she'll draw her arms into her sleeves and cross them beneath her shirt. The first few times she did it, Tate asked if he should adjust the thermostat, but she swore she wasn't cold. Today, she wears a brown tank top with a pair of bleach stains, symmetrical enough to look deliberate, below her breasts. She brings her arms into the tank top and crosses them so the tan stubs of her shoulders occupy the arm holes. She is a loudly attractive girl.

"I was the vice president of a company that shipped fruit," he says.

The following day, she stops by unexpectedly. Tate has just returned from the hospital, and is getting ready to lie down for a nap. On the way to the living room, Callie pours herself some water, drinks it at the sink, then refills the glass. Tate waits in his reclining chair. His throat burns; his eyes feel like they're filming over. He blinks them back into focus.

On the way in, Callie ran into Mr. Stavros, who asked how she knew Tate. "I told him I was posing for a portrait you were painting. I don't think he believed me. He sort of mumbled something and walked away."

Stavros is one of Tate's neighbors. "He'll probably bring it up at the next condo association meeting," he says. The words come out like freezer-burned pellets. All he wants is to sleep. He eases the chair back a little and closes his eyes.

After awhile—he may have nodded off—Callie stands up, stretches, and says, "Tate? Would you mind if I took a bath?"

He finds a towel for her and sets it on top of the toilet seat. After turning on the water, she holds up a pair of ginseng bath sachets and asks, "Can I use these?"

The sachets—Tate doesn't exactly know how they work, or if they're even intended to be used—were bought during Jeanne's redecorating. "Of course," he says.

She starts to fiddle with her tank top. He leaves, closing the door behind him.

He busies himself in the kitchen, the room of the condo farthest from the bathroom. He washes some silverware. He stands in front of the toaster waiting for two slices of raisin bread to finish. After his injections, raisin bread is still the easiest thing to eat. But raisin bread toasts quickly: if he turns his back on it for a second it'll burn. Plus the kind he buys is swirled and topped with cinnamon, difficult under the bright orange coils to tell whether it's done toasting, or hyperilluminated, or—

Callie calls his name, twice. He raises his head from the toaster, to the wall-mounted abacus, which lists slightly, and waits. As he adjusts the abacus, she says, "Come here, Tate."

"You all right?" he calls.

"No. I'm bored. Come in here and talk to me."

At the bathroom door, he listens to the faint scuffling of bath-water. "Tate," she says, "I've got an idea."

He remains still. Often he feels, when she is visiting, a great proprietary thrill of having this attractive girl in his house. The thought of her in his arms, though, of his old speckled hand on her skinny thigh, no matter how urgently summoned, defeats him. It is impossible. It's comical. It makes sense that he should become aware of his body now that it is failing, but not like this. Callie calls his name again; he stands quietly at the door. He isn't about to open it.

He goes into his bedroom and lies down. Eyes closed, he imagines being dropped into a warm patch in the center of the ocean. He sinks slowly, pulled gently down into blackening water. Sea life swims out of his way below, fills the vacant trail he leaves above. By the time he lands on the ocean floor he is asleep.

He wakes up to a darkened room, his head hot on his pillow, and Callie, apparently, is gone.

———

Stavros smokes a black cigarette by the front door of his condo when Tate returns from dinner. Thickset and facetious, he lives four units down, a brass knocker incised with his last name on the front door. "Guess who I ran into the other day," he says.

"I know, I heard," Tate says, reaching into his pocket for his house key. "She's a volunteer from the hospital."

He's disappointed by how quickly he surrenders this to Stavros, who exhales incredulously. Tate hasn't told his neighbors he's sick but somehow, all at once, they found out. Their persistence, their hungry concern: his neighbors are like birds.

"She's sharp," Stavros says. "I bet she makes very interesting conversation."

"She wants to be a writer."

Stavros laughs. Just his shoulders shake. "It will never happen," he says. "She's too concerned with the effect she is having to be a writer. But I'm sure she'll make stories everywhere she goes."

"What do you know? You've barely spoken to her."

"I watch her get out of her car," Stavros says. "Maybe she wants to make a story with you."

Tate continues on to his condo. The cigarette smoke, mixed with the taste of his dinner, leaves him nauseous. "You don't look so good," Stavros calls. "Are you feeling okay?"

Inside, Tate washes his face at the bathroom mirror. Stavros is right: his face looks ransacked, topped by a few perfunctory wisps of hair. He feels as if he's being prepared; in a few weeks he'll be perfectly bald. Without hair, he can't look at his reflection without thinking: skull.

Jeanne started wearing a wig before beginning chemotherapy. It matched her dyed auburn hair so well that for days Tate didn't know she wore it, until one late night he saw it sitting on the floor next to her nightstand. How diffidently she died! She walked around the condo watering jade plants before she went to the hospital the final time. When people asked how she was feeling, she'd say, "Fine. You?" Her only indulgence was insisting on a piece of red-velvet cake, which sat three days in the refrigerator before Tate threw it away. Her wig is still in their bedroom closet, pinned to a faceless Styrofoam head.

Over the next few weeks, the nausea returns and he notices he's losing weight. One afternoon, after waking up from a nap with a tearing sensation in his abdomen, he goes into the bathroom and coughs up a warm clot of blood, which lands below the rim of the sink, trembles, and releases a single pinkish strand of fluid.

In the lobby of the oncology ward, Tate flips through a business magazine, stopping on an article about a man who retired from a law firm, invested wisely, and became a famous yachtsman. He remembers what Callie said about hanging out in the oncology ward, and he looks around for her: twenty or so men and women, most of them older than him and staring at a television with its sound off. Callie hasn't been to the condo in more than a month, since the day of her bath. He left a message at her house and thought about calling the hospital but he didn't want to get her in trouble. He decided that his hesitancy to go into the bathroom reflected poorly on him, that his prudishness revealed his shameful intentions. Either that, or she's embarrassed she'd asked.

The lobby smells like carpet, coffee, hairspray. His arms are numb; he can taste his fillings. He wants to lay his head in the lap of the old woman next to him. She is gripping a metal walker with one hand and digging into her hive-shaped pocketbook with the other. Stuck to the crossbar of the walker is a rectangular address label. He looks down at his own lap and sees that he's squeezing the magazine so hard he's crumpled a picture of the famous yachtsman.

The spiky-haired doctor recommends a CT scan. In the tomography room a nurse unattaches the catheter from Tate's chest. He lies on a skinny vinyl table and is inserted into the scanner with his head sticking out. Orange dye drips slowly from a bottom-heavy bag. From behind him the nurse says, "Breathe deep. Okay don't breathe." Soon he feels a lukewarm surge beginning in his forehead and ending in his lap, and he's sure he's peed himself. He tries to remember what pants he has on. The nurse says, "You might be feeling something warm right now. It's the contrast moving through."

A week later, he sits on an examination table above which hangs a bumper sticker that says ♥ *Your Phlebotomist*. The doctor comes in and looks at Tate, sits down, and looks at him again. He has a clipped smudge of a mustache. "It's such a stubborn disease," he says. "We'll want to modify our approach."

The cancer has spread to Tate's lymph nodes, which are important, the doctor reminds him, to his immune system. By *modify our approach* the doctor means Tate coming to the hospital early the next morning to have his lymph nodes and a larger section of his colon removed through his abdomen. He tells Tate not to eat anything for sixteen hours before the surgery. He looks at his watch. "That gives you about seven minutes to run to the snack machine for a Snicker's." Tate hates the man for saying *Snicker's*. He stays where he is while the doctor nods some more. "From here it gets more difficult," the man says. "You probably remember from your wife." He peeks down at his notes. "Jeanne's." He peeks again. "Colon cancer."

Back at his condo he tries to think of someone to call. Jeanne's brother and his family live abroad. Tate can never figure out the country codes so he rarely talks to them anymore. He has a few friends in town but doesn't feel like burdening them with the news. He phones Callie. He imagines the phone ringing next to a bundle of postcards atop an oversized wooden spool. When her answering machine picks up, he replaces the receiver.

He decides to clean out the refrigerator. He dumps a half gallon of milk down the sink, throws away expired salad dressing and cheese. In the far back corner of the refrigerator, hidden behind a can of sweet corn, is a jar of Jeanne's favorite brown mustard. Tate pulls it out and examines the peeling label flecked with pepper: half-empty, a year past its expiration date, turning darker brown near the top of the jar. That it so outlasted Jeanne makes the mustard seem monumental, full of importance. He throws it and the can of sweet corn in the garbage. He's neither hopeful nor hopeless, but knowing that none of the condiments will be lingering around the refrigerator if something happens, waiting for him to return home, heartens him a little.

Later, the doorbell rings. Tate looks through the peephole at Callie, who removes her sunglasses and sort of purses her lips. In her arms is a brown shopping bag. Tate opens the door and she smiles, then walks past him into the kitchen. "It smells like something in here," she says.

Tate opens a window and sits in the recliner while Callie gets something to drink. He can see one bare foot, capped by the silver anklet. He wonders how casually he'd have to say, "So where have you been?" for it not to sound like a reprimand. She comes into the living room holding two glasses of pink liquid.

"Grenadine and cheap beer," she says, handing him a glass. "It tastes like soda."

Tate waits for the foam to recede before sipping it. It indeed tastes like soda, cold and cloying. He feels it traveling as a lump down his esophagus. Callie finishes hers and makes a sour face. Her hair is fastened limply behind her head, and she looks paler, more tentative. She worries the anklet by shaking her foot around. It takes Tate a few minutes to realize she's nervous.

"It's good," he says. "I'm glad you came. I was at the hospital today."

"I guess that's why I'm here then," she says.

When Tate finishes his drink, Callie goes into the kitchen and makes another. She invites Tate to sit on the couch and rests her feet on his knee. Her legs aren't heavy. She confesses that, except for Tate, she's tired of all her friends. They just want to whine about how much they regret this and that. She's sick of it. They're so *uninteresting*. Clearly, *uninteresting*, in her opinion, is the worst thing someone can be. Her feet move around atop his knees randomly. She's considering quitting the hospital, but she wants to sleep with a doctor first, ideally a surgeon. Surgeons, she hears, are thorough. Surgeons have very clever hands. Tate studies a pair of silk fans clipped to the opposite wall, Jeanne's final flourish. He feels as if he's in a museum, eavesdropping on someone else's conversation. His leg has fallen asleep. "It's your turn to tell me a secret," Callie says.

Tate carefully sets his glass on the tea table, fitting it atop the wet ring it left. He says, "An old, old friend of Jeanne's had discouraged Jeanne from marrying me. She used to send Jeanne birthday cards and Christmas cards, which I'd open and black out a few words from their greeting. Like she'd write *Wishing you all the best these holidays. I sure would hate to still be living up north, wouldn't you!* And I'd black out the words to read *The holidays sure do hate to still be living you!* or something mean-spirited, and then mail the card back to her. After awhile they stopped coming."

Callie's expression confirms that this is a good, that is, an interesting-enough, secret. "Didn't they ever talk on the phone?" she asks. "I mean, even if Jeanne didn't know, I'm sure she *knew*. You know?"

"No," Tate says. "I'm pretty sure she didn't know."

Out the back window, he sees that the patio light has turned on: the sun is setting.

"What is this called again?" he asks, pointing to the empty glass.

"A Monaco. They drink them in Prague!"

She returns to the kitchen. Tate digs his fingers into the sofa's upholstery. He's angry with himself. There was no reason to mention the cards, to casually bring them up so as not to appear secret-less or uninteresting, which he supposes he is.

She returns with a glass in each hand. She asks, "Would you go without bathing for six months in exchange for $500,000?"

"Who's going to pay that much for me not to bathe?"

"Don't worry about that," she says. "The questions are supposed to make you think about how you live, what's important to you. Okay, here's another: would you live in perfect happiness for a year if at the end you wouldn't remember any of it? Why, or why not?"

"Sure," he says. "Starting right now."

"Why, or why not?"

He finishes his drink. Callie withdraws her legs and turns her head, poised to accept whatever Tate wants to unload on her. She has extremely sympathetic eyebrows. That her other friends spend their time confessing and regretting things to her doesn't surprise him. What does she expect? She's probably the only person they were moved to compose themselves around. Tonight, her eagerness seems insincere to Tate. Like earlier in the waiting room, he had the impulse to lean over, lay his head in her lap, and fall asleep. He supposes that if he'd asked, she would've allowed him to, which is partially why he didn't ask.

After a few minutes, she gets up from the couch and says, "Where are your records, Tate?"

He sits forward. "You mean pictures?"

"Albums. Record albums."

"Photo albums?"

"I think we're a little drunk. I see a record player but no records."

"Our bedroom closet," Tate says.

Callie returns with a stack of records and sets them in front of the record player. On hands and knees, she fiddles with the record player's lid and soon a woman is singing in French over the speakers. "Edith Piaf, Charles Aznavour, Jacques Brel. These are amazing," she says. "Do you speak French?"

"They belonged to Jeanne. You can have them."

She says she couldn't possibly take them. It was a casual offer, but the more reluctant she acts, the more vigorously he insists. They're just records sitting in a closet. He isn't sentimental about them, he doesn't even speak French. He'd rather someone have the records who will listen to them. Callie gives in and thanks him. They dance.

Tate's hand rests lightly on her hip. She feels small at the waist and smells like gum though he doesn't notice her chewing any. The catheter presses against his chest, pinching him. Worrying about it, he almost trips over Callie's feet, but she is a graceful dancer. Her eyes are closed. Tate knows that whatever happens tonight will be a lot like this dance: difficult for him, easy for her. This, he decides, is fine, fine.

"Aren't I a good dancer?" she says when the song ends, looking up at him. Her irises are the depthless blue of oceans in an atlas. He agrees that she is.

"Lessons," she says. She kneels down by the record player and finds another forty-five she's excited about. Tate, waiting for her to finish, can't decide what to do with his hands. "I've got an idea," she says. "I'll be right back."

A somber-sounding ballad plays, and Tate doesn't understand a word. He used to come home from work to find Jeanne with a glass of wine in the recliner, listening to her records. The wine and the music left her meek and maudlin for the rest of the evening. Tate never asked her what the songs were about; she never told him. It was a pleasant mystery. Like the two-hour walks she took after dinner, or when she spoke French in her sleep. He knew so much and so little about her.

Just as he's about to stop the record, Callie walks in wearing a charm necklace and Jeanne's auburn wig. It sits high on her head, over her hair, which is tucked beneath it. She has a long neck and, in the wig, looks like some sort of grandmother robin. It makes Tate instantly and irrationally angry. She smiles at him. "Shall we dance?"

"First why don't you take that off?"

"Hey, why don't we pretend we're on a ship crossing the Atlantic? Like I'm the ladies auxiliary seeing you off to war. We've got one night until we hit port."

"That's a bit too close to the truth. Right now, I'd really like you to take the wig off."

She steps closer to him, lifting her skinny arms to dance. "Tonight we dance, tomorrow it's *au revoir*."

He expected Callie would do something irresponsible, he was hoping for it, actually. He was prepared to give in to whatever reckless idea she had. But not this. Not crossing the Atlantic and seeing him off to war in Jeanne's wig. "Here," he says.

He grabs the wig and yanks harder than he intends. He expects to casually pull it off and toss it into the bedroom. Instead the wig shifts only slightly and Callie's neck lurches. "That hurts," she says, gripping and pushing away Tate's arm. "Let go. You're *hurting* me."

He doesn't let go. Instead he pulls harder, reasoning that once he frees the wig, she'll see why he grabbed it, and understand. He isn't able to. She squirms free and collapses on the couch, out of breath, beginning to cry. The wig has shifted sideways enough for Tate to see the pearl-white heads of the pins holding it in place.

The record ends and the needle ticks against the label before it lifts and resets. "That was not deliberate," he says.

"What's wrong then? Why did you grab me?" She sits up, pulls the pins out of the wig carefully, one by one, and sets them and the wig next to her. Her hair gleams in contrast, as if she pulled off a scab. "What's wrong?" she repeats.

That she has no idea she's done anything inappropriate—looking around the bedroom closet for something to put on, settling on Jeanne's wig—seems to Tate unforgivably arrogant. "I'm sick," he says. "No matter how much I want to, I'm not getting better."

She stands up and gathers the empty glasses from the tea table.

"You don't have to do that," he says.

He follows her into the kitchen, where she tucks the half-empty grenadine bottle into the shopping bag among beer cans. She won't look at him. "We were having fun," she tells the bag.

"Take the records," Tate says. He sees no good way to stop her from leaving, but thinks he can delay her a little longer. "Take whatever looks interesting."

To his surprise Callie finds another shopping bag, returns to the living room, and fills it with records. It takes about two minutes. "Your nose is bleeding," she says on the way out. The usual concern in her voice is missing. If it had been there, he wouldn't have recognized it, but its absence is far easier to identify. From the kitchen window he watches her get into her black car and drive away.

In the living room he holds a wet paper towel to his nose. With his head back he can see the top bookshelf arrayed with knick-knacks: a pair of Confucius figurines, saki cups around a tiny decanter, a Zen waterfall that, when plugged in, makes serene cascading noises. Jeanne, Jeanne, Jeanne. The blood pools along his palate. The record continues to play.

When the bleeding stops, Tate returns the wig to the closet. It is stored on a Styrofoam head, a bare white egg on a stand, not a head at all really, something designed with a single purpose in mind. Tate pins the wig to it, positioning the wig with the label toward the back. It makes the egg more head-like. "Placeholder," he says to the egg.

He isn't tired so he goes into the living room to listen to Jeanne's records, forgetting that Callie has left with them. There is just the forty-five on the turntable, which ends and resets every few minutes. He is thinking about Callie's question: a year of perfect happiness after which he wouldn't remember anything. The more he listens to the record, the more he likes the notion of a year of perfect happiness forgotten. Not the anticipation of one to come, but the idea that one might have existed in his past. *A year of perfect happiness,* just the sound of it, a single year locked away from the years before and the years after it, happiness unburdened by nostalgia, perfect . . .

In the morning, the record is still playing. Tate packs a small suitcase, locks the door to his condo, and drives himself to the hospital.

A
Statement
of
Purpose

───────────
▅▅▅▅

The two of them, Ben and Adria, meeting in a
manatee pool. The pool, part of Manatee Encounter, is edged by
smooth-topped coquina rocks on which elderly couples sun themselves, apparently tired of communing with the lumbering sea life.
"Nature's speed bumps," one of the men says. The elderly couples
watch the rehabilitated manatees swim around and around beneath Ben and Adria, the sole humans in the pool, who tread water
in black life jackets. "Mauled by boats, all of them," one of the
wives says.

Ben is waiting for the manatees to resurface. Below him he can
see the animals' dim dun shapes, prehistorically slow. He has been

considering trying to mount the big cow they call Michelle, but he figures the handlers would have a way of humiliating him publicly if he did. He thinks, Men throughout history have discovered animals and ridden them. "If I could rig up a water-safe harness," he says aloud. "A proper saddle, I mean."

"What then?" Adria says.

He turns his attention to this woman with orangish water-slicked-back hair. Her face is thin and sunburned and plain. "The earliest explorers mistook manatees for mermaids," she says. "Ever since, there's been sort of a love-hate thing with the manatee."

She smiles, becomes embarrassed, smiles wider. Her top teeth are crooked, a trait Ben finds instantly, unequivocally sexy. The teeth make him want to make her laugh. "What I think the manatee needs to do is make itself available to be ridden," he says. "America loves an animal it can ride. You think anyone's going to *eat* a horse, or plow through a herd of them in a Chris-Craft? People have incredibly complex feelings for the horse."

She laughs. Treading water in front of her, he thinks of bad girls gone schoolgirl, schoolgirls gone bad. The water is warm, which is how the manatees, down below them, bothering the water with their slowness, like it.

Ben likes propositions of all kinds, including ones he knows he'll never act on, *especially* ones he knows he'll never act on. He is a man with a high tolerance for possibility. His life jacket, too small for him, makes him look like a well-meaning imposter. His Adam's apple bobs above and below the water's surface. A manatee appears close behind Adria, sneezes out a spray of water, and he gets a warm and uncomplicated feeling. He says, "Here's the part where I ask a question and you promise not to be spooked off."

She promises without pause. He thinks of the best way to construct what he wants to ask, so the surprise of the request will overshadow most possible menace. The important thing in a situation like this is to phrase the request as nonchalantly, as delicately as possible. He says, "Can I ride you?"

Ben calling ten minutes after dropping her off at her house. They've been to see a movie about a group of veterans in wheelchairs who solve murders. Ben's voice sounds huskier, more determined than earlier. "I need to know something," he says. "Don't think I'm crazy."

Before Adria has a chance to answer, he says, "Will you stick around if I get paralyzed?"

Adria has the brief suspicion this isn't Ben on the telephone but somebody else. She says, "Of course I will."

"Paraplegia, I mean, waist down. I'm in a wheelchair but can change my clothes and shave, comb my hair. You won't need to do any of that. Digestive function: normal. Sexual function: normal. Listen, from the get-go I'm determined not to let my affliction slow me down. I'm active in wheelchair sports, advocacy groups, select political campaigns. Soon we're going to forget all about this."

"I'm not going anywhere."

Ben says, "I'll definitely be putting a mini license plate on the back of the wheelchair. Something uplifting. For the kids."

She is afraid to tell her friends about Ben. They'll ask questions she doesn't know the answers to. Marta and Sarah, Melissa, Amanda, Jennifer, Rachel, and Steph. Adria's friends are pretty and she is not. They meet men who work in marketing, men who enjoy specific, tangible things, like cunnilingus and microbrewed beer. Ben has never really talked about what he does for a living.

"If I lost function in my arms I could mouth-paint," he says.

She likes him past any conceivable explanation of why she likes him. She wakes up in the morning with a head full of plans. She wants to relearn the trumpet, relearn Spanish. She's been thinking about having herself refitted for braces.

"I *know* I'd do something exceptional," he says.

She has known him two weeks.

Ben and his policy of giving a woman a coffee mug, handing it to her, unwrapped, at the end of the eighth date and carefully monitoring her response. The way a woman reacts when handed an unwrapped coffee mug tells him much of what he needs to know about her. An overly favorable reaction toward the mug is not ideal. It shows a false congeniality, a graciousness out of proportion to the gift, because what kind of gift is a coffee mug? When the congeniality is exhausted, where will they be then? A negative reaction to the mug, this is closer to adequate. Yes, simple honesty is what Ben is looking for. Or, failing that, dishonest restraint rendered plausibly. Actually, Ben isn't sure what he is looking for.

In Adria's car, parked in front of Ben's apartment, he talks about the Tampa Bay Buccaneers. He has been a loyal fan of the team since 1976, the year they went 0–14, and now that they have changed stadiums and uniforms and have won the Super Bowl, he finds himself discontented. "I could *understand* them when they were losers," he says. "Now, even the players' names, *Griese, Pittman, Alstott,* they sound like action movies, like dudes in action movies. The new coach works sixteen-hour days. A *football* coach working *sixteen-hour days* . . ." He trails off to let himself stew temporarily in the sweet betrayal of the Tampa Bay Buccaneers' success. This is one of his favorite things to do.

"You're a friend of the underdog," Adria says. "If you weren't, you would've never been out there swimming with the manatees. And we would've never met. It's a good—"

In the middle of her sentence, Ben reaches into his backpack and presents her with the mug. Adria, caught on the end of a word, appraises the mug noncommittally. Her eyes shift from it to Ben to it. "It's a good characteristic," she finishes.

Returning her attention to the mug she says, "I don't drink coffee."

"That's okay. It should work with other liquids."

"I'd been thinking about starting something new, I mean."

She stares at the mug and smiles. Lately Ben has begun forcing himself to look away from her teeth when she bares them, they're so alluring. The crooked teeth are an unfair advantage. What happened to him that he's now so moved by imperfection? Bad football teams, women with crooked teeth, with leg bruises, on crutches, women in wigs, very short women, women with poor posture, with lazy eyes, with neck braces, arm slings, stretch marks, missing fingers, acne, rosacea, psoriasis, mangled toes, arm fat, women with skin grafts, burns, and other scars, scars, in particular those glorious raised red keloid scars.

When Adria is finished smiling, her bottom lip snags on her tooth. To Ben, turning back to her, this is just too damn much. He surrenders and kisses her, running his tongue along the jagged back gate of her teeth. He smells a soapy smell as Adria swallows deeply and holds her breath—she always does this when they kiss. It lends the kisses a solemn and metered aspect.

He did not monitor her reaction to the mug closely enough. Before he gets out of the car to go into his apartment, he looks at her one more time. Her nose is treaded with blackheads, football-textured. Her hair, tinted a pumpkin color, is too short; her eyes, too closely set. From a distance her irises blend with her pupils and are as black and inert as an umlaut.

She has him.

"Night," he says, reaching for the door handle.

"Ben," she says. She leans over, kisses him on the cheek, and pauses, staring at the mark her lipstick made. She says, "You're perfect."

He smiles. ". . . said the spider to the fly," he says.

Adria wondering, When is he going to ride me? There are many things about which she cannot think rationally. Sex is one of these things. She's had it on nine occasions, each time with a different stranger who groped her for a few minutes before tearing off her clothes and seesawing atop her, emitting low reptile grunts. A few of them called her *baby* as in *baby, yeah, that's right, baby, oh, you like how I'm deep-dogging you, baby?* And made her long for a scrap, however brief, of honest communion, like between parent and baby, not these sorry snake pit pump-ruts. By the third time, she found that if she remained absolutely still, the operation ended soon enough. The worst part, though, came next: post-coital conversation, during which Adria's fantasies swayed between the homicidal and the suicidal. A man who talks about his penis in the third person, referring to it as *he*, is, to Adria's mind, capable of any imaginable atrocity, and should be injured and banished. A man who knows how and when to shut up is a comrade for life, even if she thinks she'll never see him again. Especially if she thinks she'll never see him again.

Contrary to his proposal in the manatee pool, Ben has yet to make a discernible advance toward riding her. His tentativeness pleases her: it shows he is less unhinged than she previously supposed, that he is in possession of some gallant logic. His tentativeness also worries her: maybe he isn't interested in riding her. Maybe the proposal was strictly figurative, like the song, "Love Train." As a teenager, Adria answered a survey in a *Seventeen* magazine called "Is Your Boy a Cold-Timing Charlie?" with multiple-choice questions like, "Does he use tongue when he's kissing you? If yes, how much tongue?"

In high school, Adria's mother told her that she, Adria, was just going through some awkward years, that she would grow up to be beautiful when the acne cleared and she figured out how to apply makeup. Adria had been a striking baby, her mother assured her. People used to come up to baby Adria and say, "Now *that* is a handsome baby." Adria didn't care. Early on, she noticed how pretty girls bloomed and blanched from being stared at. It was the end of their internal life, beauty being its own kind of minor celebrity in the beach town where she grew up. Everything about these girls, women now, some of whom Adria has remained friends with, is turned outward. When she's with them, Adria watches men watch them. The men try to erase the women's advantage with a proprietary, predatory regard that Adria knows she could never shoulder. Her friends seem to ignore it away.

Why didn't Ben's proposition in the manatee pool seem sinister? Adria was going to answer, "Hop on," but before she could, one of the manatee handlers appeared atop the rocks and said, "Time's up, lovebirds." Writing his phone number on a Manatee Encounter cocktail napkin, Ben told her he liked the sound of it: *lovebirds.*

She learns things about him, slowly and almost always by accident. He'll let slip a tentative memory here, a preference or prejudice there. He likes watching nature shows on television. He is scared of wasps and bees. His father, retired in Arizona, used to work as a librarian, and Ben reads all the time. One of his favorite books is called *How We Die,* written in excruciatingly clear-eyed detail by a surgeon hoping to demystify and deromanticize death. The surgeon describes a time when he pulled the heart out of a cardiac-arresting man's chest with the intention of massaging the heart back to life, and instead watched it fibrillate and die in his hands. Ben reads a passage aloud to Adria, where the surgeon compares the fibrillating heart to a "wet, jellylike bagful of hyperactive worms."

The two of them are sitting face-to-face on a velour couch in Ben's living room. Their legs are interlocked and each time Ben pauses to carefully enunciate one of the more clinical terms—*thoracotomy, pericardium, ventricular*—Adria feels a jellylike hyperactivity in her own thorax. She listens and plays with the hair on his calves, trying to nap it into balls by rubbing it in little circles. Ben has such pristine leg fur, soft as lanugo. Adria rubs, rubs. What else is good about Ben? He has big red lips. His good humor is inscribed on his face. He is erratically irreverent. Much of the time he appears to be thinking aloud, trying to arrive at what he wants to say by saying it. He doesn't banter. He doesn't volley. He isn't trying to promote a public notion of his own intelligence.

He is kind to her. He likes her.

Ben reads, "At the time the fibrillating patient's life came to its abrupt end, the outcome of his heart's misbehavior was inescapable."

Behind him, a shaded standing lamp casts an almondy glow over the couch. Adria finds herself passing in and out of attentiveness, still rubbing and staring at Ben's leg hair. When is he going to ride her? His body is slim and unobtrusive. Often he smells like the beach. He probably looks excellent in formal wear, or at the bedside of a dying relative, or captaining a boat, or leaning on his elbow in front of a campfire, or holding a newborn baby, or tied naked to a La-Z-Boy. His toes are unbelievable.

"There are few reliable accounts," he reads, "of the ways in which we die."

His voice, his voice is like some vital jungle thing.

He will leave her. He is going to leave her.

————

Alone at home, Ben watching a TV show about manatees. "When Florida's first explorers encountered what we now call the manatee," the narrator intones, "they were drunk on rum and orange wine. Some of them actually jumped into the water and went after the hulking animals."

A story too preposterous to be untrue, Ben thinks, though Adria never mentioned that the explorers were drunk. Ben is glad to know they were. He hopes the explorers stayed drunk among the mermaids, delaying for a while full awareness of the gentle but unlovely sea cow, the forfeiture of possibility . . .

Adria calling her friend Melissa, who teaches kindergarten and collects stuffed animals, to tell her that she's been to Dr. Lentz, an orthodontist. Melissa had braces a few years ago to correct a slight, slight underbite. She answers the phone, "Who dis?" Adria can tell she's in one of her jovial moods. After the preliminary niceties are out of the way, Melissa starts in with the lingo—the jovial moods are always accompanied by the lingo. It goes something like: "Aw snap. Peep this: you gots to *chill*."

"I can't remember if they hurt or not," Adria says. "Are they going to hurt?"

"Girl, nuh-uh, not a bit."

This is Melissa's way of joking with Adria and their other friends when she's in a jovial mood. It is her only exceptional characteristic.

"Lentz creeps me out with that singing. And the other patients, all of us in the same room together."

"You a trip, girl. You a maiden voyage."

Those who endeavor to be funny and are not are a sorry membership. Adria is thinking again about Ben, who seldom fails to be funny when he is trying to. It confers him with an immediate dignity Melissa will never know. Adria can hear her breathing heavily on the other end of the line.

"We're all, like, so *totally* glad you're doing this," Melissa says, back to normal.

Adria hasn't told Ben about the braces. She wants to surprise him. What does Melissa mean by *we*? Adria feels hastily discussed by her friends, manhandled. She says, "We?"

Ben at the flea market, studying an Amish woman behind a booth that offers a selection of puppies for sale. A handwritten sign, hanging from the back of a minivan with Pennsylvania license plates, says, Amish Puppies are Better'n Mennonite Puppies, Ask Why. Next to the woman a half-dozen or so Amish kids, maybe hers, are behind a metal cage, playing with puppies. The kids hold up the puppies to anyone who passes near the cage. They babble with natural salesmanship while the puppies squirm in their arms. The woman, wearily seated in a wooden folding chair, seems subordinated by their happiness. Ben is moved by her posture of defeat, but doesn't think the interest is strictly sexual. Maybe it is. Restraint makes her cenotaphic, emptily tempting. She wears a formless frock, and her face, crowned by a simple lace bonnet, is as unexceptional as a bowl of butter.

What does he know about the Amish? He knows they build barns and make bell harnesses for those Clydesdales in beer commercials. And that they're required to leave the farm the year they turn sixteen, to cavort with other Amish teenagers in rented apartments with whiskey and satellite TV to see if they prefer it over the barn-building and the bell-harness-making. Ben thinks the Amish are fascinating and ridiculous. This woman, she's maybe twenty-five, thirty at the oldest, wasting the day away selling Amish puppies, wilting at night under the pious girth of some Jebediah or Ezekiel, who waits until she's fallen asleep to crawl over the two-by-four they've nailed down the middle of their homemade bed for modesty . . .

Ben forces himself to think about Adria.

Today he is trying to find a gift for her at the flea market. A real gift, one that he hopes will serve as a statement of purpose. Unlike the mug, which Adria has taken up coffee drinking to make use of, Ben intends this gift to err on the side of the dramatic. Ben is not going to leave Adria. He no longer thinks about leaving Adria.

When they are not together, Ben notices that the memory of her is slow to summon, but once it does, for the rest of the day he carries an image of her slanted loveliness around with him. She has recently tried to dye her hair back to its natural color, which is a kind of late-bruise brownish red, and she has begun to wear nail polish and outlandish jewelry, and Ben has a hard time pinning down the general effect. They've been together nearly four months and still he has not ridden her. They haven't discussed the not-riding; they haven't discussed the not-discussing-the-not-riding. They talk about . . . what is it Ben and Adria talk about? They talk about Adria's friends. They talk about the books they read. They talk about things they've done and things, with the exception of riding, they want to do. They talk about and about.

Ben envisions giving her the statement-of-purpose gift at his apartment, the two of them quietly agreeing on its appropriateness and generosity, and then him leading her into his bedroom for him to finally, alas, ride her. He pictures wrapping paper on the floor, a general frolicking. And later, Adria wrapped in one of his towels standing in a lighted doorway.

What is good about Adria? She is unselfishly sentimental. She is unafraid of silence or whether the stories she tells reflect poorly on her. She is far more respectful of others than they are of her. Her sincerity is contagious, unaffected, becoming. Her interest in clothing is minimal. Her crooked teeth have gone from a distinct alluring oddity to just another element of her face. She is no longer a novelty. To him, she is beautiful.

But what gift? What will say what Ben cannot?

Ben starts over to the booth. Up close, he notices that the children are exquisite. There are five of them, three girls, two boys, each identically wheat-faced and farm-radiant, like little collectible dolls. Standing outside the metal cage that houses them and the puppies, Ben is hesitant to talk to them, afraid he'll somehow corrupt them with his urgency.

One of the little girls notices him and hands him a puppy. It tenses when it lands in Ben's grip, briefly, then relaxes again. He holds it out in front of him with both hands like an offering. The puppy, some kind of husky or chow mixture, is cosmically soft and white with a black spot on its side, eyes tightly shut, quivering, barely past the point of being born. The puppy has been born, but it doesn't know it's been born. Its dream-mind has not yet surrendered from sleep. This, to Ben, is a wonderful, a near-religious, notion. He leans down and carefully rests his face in the dog's soft stomach fur.

"Why are Amish puppies better'n Mennonite puppies?" he asks the little girl.

The girl shrugs. She has picked up another puppy and is looking around for somebody to unload it on. "Mommy, why are our puppies better?" she asks the woman in the folding wooden chair.

The woman, staring at her shoes, doesn't look up. "Tell the man those aren't the better puppies."

The Amish woman's teeth are crooked, Ben notices.

"She says these aren't the better puppies."

"I heard her," Ben says to the girl. "The man can hear you," he says to the woman, who's about ten feet away. The woman doesn't acknowledge him; she continues to imperially scowl at her scuffed black shoes. "I said I can hear you," he repeats, louder this time. And suddenly he hates this woman and her puritan apathy for souring his moment with the puppy.

Ben looks down again at the little animal sleeping in his hands. It has given itself to him totally. He thinks, Nobody needs to tell us we've been born. One day we just wake up. He asks the little girl, who has handed off the puppy and is reaching for another, "So how do you like being Amish so far?"

Back at his apartment, he calls Adria. "Look here, lovebird," he says. "How about coming over?" He has bought a dog leash, dog collar, dog bowls, dog bed, dog toys, dog food. The Amish puppy is asleep on the red tile floor by Ben's feet.

"I have an appointment," she says. "I'll come over after work tomorrow. I have a surprise for you."

"I like surprises," he says.

Adria beneath the wall-to-wall ceiling mirror in Dr. Lentz's office, six chairs arranged in a half moon around a marble island of sinks. Adria, fully reclined, can see the chairs, the sink, Lentz, and the two assistants tightening wires and attaching rubber bands. Chair 1: boy with jet black hair. Chair 2: boy in a hooded sweatshirt giggling at something, maybe her. Chair 3: Adria. Chair 4: girl with her mouth pried open, being worked on currently by Lentz and one of the assistants. From time to time the girl's eyes meet Adria's in the mirror. Chair 5: boy in wrestling sneakers having his wires tightened by the other assistant. Chair 6: very young girl who Adria overheard was having tiny spikes installed to correct a lisp.

Adria is waiting with a plastic harness in her mouth for her teeth to dry so Lentz can brush them with glue and apply brackets. Finished with the girl in chair 4, he walks to the sinks and washes his hands. Adria is frightened of Dr. Lentz. He inspects the mouth of the boy with jet black hair and says, "Rebrush!" and the boy gets up from the chair and sullenly walks over to the brushing station on the opposite side of the sinks, where an assistant shows him the proper way to brush. Lentz goes from chair to sink to chair, taking off and putting on disposable gloves, and crooning along with the rock muzak that plays from an unseen speaker. The orthodontist sings tough-faced, no joy in his delivery.

He and one of the assistants pull up stools next to Adria's chair. The assistant readies the pliers and glues while Lentz is singing, "Choke me in the shallow water," a song Adria recognizes. Her mind measures the activity, but doesn't analyze it. Lentz's hands, covered in white latex, are in her mouth. The assistant holds a curved tube firmly against the inside of Adria's cheek to suck saliva, probing around now and then to get at every drop. Lentz brushes the glue on and applies the brackets. His fingers delicately work their way around her teeth, attending to each of them. Watching in the mirror above as Lentz and his assistant lean over her, she feels scooped into, plumbed. "Do not swallow," the assistant says. The kids all look in the ceiling mirror, at her. The boy in the hooded sweatshirt is still giggling. Lentz sings, "I know what I know if you know what I mean." His hazel eyes, darting behind his thick-lensed glasses as he brushes the glue on and applies the brackets, suggest something panicking under ice.

Adria assures herself, They're fixing me. They're making me prettier.

"All set, you," Lentz says, patting the top of her thigh roughly. He's threaded the brackets with a wire, which is fixed into place with rubber bands. Adria runs her tongue along the outside of her teeth, top and bottom: little wire trestles from tooth to tooth.

As Dr. Lentz walks back to the island of sinks, the assistant says, "He's no prince, but he's a genius with teeth." She, too, pats Adria's thigh. "You should spit now, honey."

Adria with a bottle of wine, knocking on Ben's front door, her nod to propriety. Ben answers in a T-shirt and shorts. "Well, well, well," he says. She wears a red and white striped sundress and black cloth ballerina slippers. Her ankles are tan. Ben moves out of the doorway and makes an exaggerated welcome sweep with his arm, stopping her to kiss her before she walks by. Something different about her hair, a new pair of turquoise earrings, eye shadow maybe. She sits down on his sofa, setting the wine bottle by her feet. Ben leaves the door open and walks over to the sofa. Adria is trying not to smile, trying not to smile. She smiles. Metal shine of brackets and wires, she looks at him with a hopeful but wounded expression. "Surprise," she says. She has to snap her lips forward to get them back over the braces.

Ben sits next to her on the sofa. He wipes his hands on his shorts, says, "Open back up," trying to sound genial, but it comes out irritable. He feels himself getting impatient. "Let's see what you, uh, got in there," trying genial, sounding irritable.

She smiles again, opens her mouth. Ben leans closer. Reaching into her mouth, he runs his finger slowly along the jagged brackets, a quarter-inch thick, working right now to correct her smile. He wants to hurry up and reach a consensus about them but all he can summon is a knee-jerk dislike toward the change. He liked her crooked teeth, he was *used* to her crooked teeth. Now it's the braces; after that, it will be the effect of the braces. In high school he was fond of several girls with braces. He thinks of them now: Jenny Ware, Missy Thompson, Darla Edinger. When the braces came off, their teeth looked like piano keys, long and straight. Adria is waiting for him to speak.

"Well, they're something," he says.

She snaps her lips forward, covering the braces.

"So, why now?" he says.

"I've been wanting to get them for awhile. I don't know. I thought it seemed like a good time." The braces make her voice sound thin and nasally. More change. "You don't like them."

She shrugs and sighs. Her hesitancy, familiar to Ben, settles him down a little, although he still can't come up with anything judicious to say about the braces. Why don't his biases bear scrutiny? He should love the braces. He stands up and says, "Follow me."

Ben leading Adria by the hand into his bedroom, kicking a yellow squeaky toy out of the way. Adria tries not to anticipate disappointment. Ben tries to soften his impatience. Adria takes off Ben's shirt. Ben takes off Adria's dress. A gentle undoing. Adria's hands, Ben's voice. Slowness, Ben opens and closes his eyes, quickness, mutual regard, sweat, silence, silence. Aloneness. Dissolving daylight. Glow in the dark stars and planets on Ben's ceiling, like a little boy's room. Adria thinks about her friends again, rubbing Ben's chest hair in little circles, allowing herself a single comment. "That was a nice surprise." The sound of sprinklers, cicadas. Ben thinks: the puppy.

Ben scrambling out of bed, searching the floor for his clothes. Adria had been half dreaming, half wondering how she would describe this evening to her friends. The glow in the dark stars, the sprinklers. Ben is leaving the room. First comes the shift, then the awareness of the shift. She feels lost already. She feels like calling out, "Freeze," and stopping things. Ben returns.

"I put it in the bathroom," he says. "I was going to tell you to close your eyes and then I'd bring it out to you. It's gone. I forgot to shut the front door."

He sits with his back to her on the foot of the bed and tells her about the puppy, where he found it, his idea about it not yet knowing it's been born. Adria is having a hard time following him. She tries to sense where the evening is heading, wants to meet it before it gets there. Leaning over the edge of the bed, she finds her bra and struggles to put it on beneath the covers. "Let's find it," she says. "What's its name?"

"I haven't given it a name."

"What's it look like?"

"It's black with a white spot. It's cute and small, I don't know, it's Amish." His voice cracks on the last word.

The two get dressed and go outside to search for the puppy. The apartment is surrounded by chinaberry shrubs that Ben kneels on his hands and knees to search under. Another starless night, the dumb glow of a full moon all over the sky. Adria calls, "Come on, puppy, puppy, puppy." She looks down at her dress and sees that she's put it on inside out. The roots of her teeth are starting to hurt. "Puppy, puppy, puppy," she says. She wants to give the dog a name, but thinks that might somehow doom it. Watching Ben scramble around beneath the bushes, she tries to stem the pain by holding her hand to her mouth.

After another half hour of searching, the two go back inside the apartment. Adria sits down on the sofa, the bottle of wine still on the red tile floor in front of her, unopened. She had planned to say, "Surprise," and then smile, not the other way around. First comes expectation, then disappointment. She closes her eyes. Her teeth are really hurting her now, a lively pain. She can feel each tooth tugged, and tugging back, the straight ones helping to align the crooked ones, tugging them down and allowing them to slip into place. It has always been this way. She was a striking baby, her mother used to say. In a few years, men are gonna be chasing after you, just you wait. She waited. Her friends still call men *boys*, call successful dates *sleepovers*. The crooked ones tug and tug but the straight ones are tugging harder. Just you wait. She waited for years and then one came.

Ben turns the stereo on and sits down. Adria feels his sweaty arm come to rest around her shoulders, holding her next to him. He is breathing damply and heavily. Each breath seems to pull her a little closer to him, under him. "Well, well," he says. "Look what we have here."

Adria opens her eyes and looks at Ben, who is pointing to the corner of the living room.

The puppy. Sitting up in its purple bed in the corner, trying to lick itself awake. Yawning and shivering and opening its eyes. Ben says, "It was here all this time." Lifting his arm from her, he moves toward the puppy. He picks it up. "You nearly fooled us."

Adria nodding. Adria giving it a name.

Space

The winter Ray finished high school, his grandmother wrote a letter to the community college asking for him to
be admitted, assuring them that he was a smart boy who had been
distracted in high school by an ailing mother. Of course the community college accepted anyone, but when the admittance letter
arrived his grandmother acted as if she'd won a complex appeal.
"The power of reason!" she said, showing him the acceptance letter. "Now it's time to act like somebody." At the dining room table,
she began writing another letter, her hair tied into a long, gray-
streaked braid, the only way he'd ever seen her wear it.

"Thesaurus," she said. Ray went to her room and found the
leather-bound book on the dressing table beneath a rhinestone-

studded hand mirror. He set it on the dining room table next to her and she asked, "Do you have the shoes I bought you? The inoffensive ones from Sears?"

She turned her head sideways, pen poised in the air, and waited for an answer. "Yes," he said. "They may be too small. I haven't worn them in a while."

"Course not, you aristocrat." She slid the thesaurus closer. "But you can't start college in those. Those shoes aren't fit for selling tires."

He looked down at the red canvas high-tops his grandmother disliked so much. Clown shoes, she called them, the shoes of someone poor imitating someone rich imitating someone poor. His grandmother startled and fascinated him. He'd long given up trying to match her enthusiasm, content to take her side of an argument instead of asserting his own. Course the red shoes were foolish. Course he'd start college in his funeral shoes.

She used the thesaurus whenever she wrote a letter. A few weeks ago, when she began writing to the community college, she'd said the same thing: "Thesaurus," like a surgeon calling for a scalpel. When he gave it to her, she found the page she wanted, then quickly scanned it with her finger. "Bereaved," she had said, closing the book. "That's exactly what you are."

He had lived at Coral Grove sporadically since he was sixteen, moving in for good after his mother died. It was an all-seniors condo flanked by shuffleboard courts and an asphalt lot full of handicapped parking spaces. Management made an exception for Ray because his grandmother, vigorous, impatient, seventy-one years old, was known around town for writing letters. Many of the letters began: "I have never been so outraged in my life." Perhaps they feared being the subject of one of them.

His mother had died slowly of lymphoma more than a year ago. His grandmother went without Ray to see her the day she died. The first time he asked what his mother had said, his grandmother answered, "She expressed concerns regarding the family line." The second time he asked: "She called for a hot-glue gun." The third time: "Are you writing a book, Ray?"

Her favorite story regarding his mother was the one about her being afraid of thunder, and how she would come to sleep between her and Ray's grandfather whenever it started to rain. His mother would stretch out her arms and legs in her sleep, and it was like sleeping—and his grandmother always saved this for last—with a swastika. She told it again and again, an automatic response when someone brought up the topic of sleep, thunder, or children. Ray figured she still told the story so much because it had nothing, really, to do with his mother.

He started community college in the spring. His classes were in the General Education building, whose name was painted in black lettering on one of the second-floor windows, abbreviated to read GENED. On the first day of Astronomy, the teacher shining a flashlight on his own waxen face to demonstrate something, Ray studied his classmates' shoes. Nearly everyone in the room, including the teacher, was wearing flip-flops. Ray wore the tasseled loafers his grandmother had bought him at Sears for his mother's funeral. She'd waited for the salesman to leave to tell Ray his mother had died. He hated the shoes. He could barely look at them without getting angry, so he tried not to look at them.

"Think of all that potential energy!" the teacher was saying.

A few girls manipulated the flip-flops between their toes, tapping the stiff rubber soles rhythmically against their heels in stubborn unison. One girl, whom Ray recognized from the smokers' wall in high school, had toenails the color of cough drops. When she noticed him looking at them, she curled in her toes and, like a bird taking flight, retracted her feet beneath the desk. *Not for you*, he imagined her thinking. Before the teacher dismissed class, he said, "Next week get ready to talk about intra-planetary pull." Ray looked at his notes. He had written "20 billion stars?"

On the bus bench, he chewed a piece of gum next to a girl dandling a baby in her lap. "James does not like green cars," the girl said to the baby. "James does not like white trucks. What does James like?" Ray saw that she was practicing from a language primer on the bench next to her. The baby pawed at the air and laughed. Their mutual regard, the girl's hopeful-sounding voice as she recited her lessons, relaxed him. He reached into his backpack and offered a piece of gum to the girl, who shook her head uncertainly and said, "No thank you." She wore what looked like a doll's dress, with cross stitches just below her breasts, and was lankly, raggedly attractive. He offered the piece of gum to the baby and the girl said, "I have doubts."

On the bus home, the girl and her baby sat behind him. He kept his backpack on and sat slouched forward, elbows propped on his knees. He studied himself in the rearview mirror, his face knot-rigid, comically sour. Behind him, he could see the baby perched in the mother's lap, waving to herself in the mirror. The mom looked to be nineteen or twenty, no wedding ring, no watch. In the mirror, Ray watched the baby's hand lift slowly into the air. He felt fingers on the base of his neck, gently tapping his topmost vertebra. He turned around and the baby was leaning over the back of the bench and smiling, wide enough for Ray to see tiny hollows in the roof of her mouth where her teeth would be. "She like you," the mother said.

Ray reached out and took the baby's hand, which was warm and seemed to wilt slightly when he touched it, and said, "Good to meet you."

The girl told Ray what she could about the baby, whose name was Martha, or Marta. She born in midnight. She eight months old. She eat pretty good. She sleep not so good. Ray sat sideways on his seat and browsed the baby's face as the mother spoke, trying not to appear uncomfortable. The baby had the exaggerated features of a highly magnified insect. Eyes so black they looked irisless.

"What do you study?" the mother asked.

Astronomy, Algebra, Intro to Writing, Study Skills. "Space," he said. It was a joke of his grandmother's, one that made sense only in response to someone asking, "What are you taking up?" which no one ever did.

"We study *Ingles*," the girl said. "It's hard, you know? We study James and his cars. James hate most of his cars."

She and Ray looked at each other. He saw curiosity in her expression, unconcealed interest, he was sure of it. Above the curved flare of her nostril glittered a nearly imperceptible gemstone. "Your English sounds good," he said.

But the girl was standing up to pull the stop cable, expertly holding the baby on her jutted-out hip in a way that allowed her to use both hands. With her left she straightened the dress along the inner part of her thigh where Ray's stare had landed. "Say bye-bye now. Bye-bye."

Ray, not realizing at first she was talking to Martha, or Marta, said bye-bye. She stopped at the front of the bus to ask the driver a question before getting off. The driver shrugged indifferently, the baby started coughing, and the girl debarked. Watching her cross the street, he felt oddly protective of her. She held up her daughter's arm and used it to wave to him, or to the bus, from the other side of the street. He held up his hand.

A few weeks after the semester began, twice in one day his grandmother referred to what she called her *expiration*. In the morning she said, "Two things worry me about expiring." But then she didn't say what the two things were.

And, later in the afternoon: "Wait a few days after my expiration to sell my furniture for kindling."

This came just after he returned from class and the two were sitting in lounge chairs by Coral Grove's shuffleboard courts. A woman in a natty blue caftan pushed her disk and together Ray and his grandmother watched it glide across the green concrete into the space marked *Off*. The woman smacked the front of her thigh, displeased.

"Why are you telling me this?" Ray asked her. "Do you actually think I'd sell your furniture?"

"No. But the idea grows funnier and funnier, the way a word does when repeated too many times. *Antelope. Antelope. Antelope.*" His grandmother looked blithely happy in her chair. Her cloudy blue eyes were hidden behind a pair of huge prescription sunglasses that added a slight indignity to her appearance, like a plastic bag snagged on a statue. "You know the last thing your mother said, Ray, the very last thing? She told one of her doctors, 'Go look for me outside, why don't you.' It was wonderfully executed."

"That's not what you told me last time."

"I've told you a lot of nothing," she said. *Go look for me outside* was his grandmother's sense of humor, not his mother's, who thought people falling down was funny, and little else. His grandmother was a performer. Often, in elevators, when feeling overly girdled by strangers, she would say, "Sure is crowded in here. One grenade could kill us all," which would usually be followed by shrugging laughter from those around her.

"I've always been poor in the sincerity department," she said. "But mine, I think, is an honest insincerity."

The woman on the shuffleboard court switched sides—apparently she was playing against herself—and Ray's grandmother began telling a story he'd heard before, the one about his mother waiting until nearly her second birthday to speak. One night she pointed to the man dancing on television and said *Elvis*. The stories his grandmother told were as familiar to him as the silver-gilt tea sets and etched crystal and starched tablecloths with holiday themes she kept in the dining room hutch. The stories were a collection of high points, connected by indistinct in-between times that lasted from punch line to punch line. The one about the police horse biting her, the one about Ray's grandfather getting drunk at a Christmas Eve party and forgetting to put presents under the tree. She didn't retell the story to demonstrate that his grandfather was thoughtless, or a drunk; it was just something funny he did once.

"Never waves," she said, nodding to a patch of palmetto grass where Zimmer, another tenant at Coral Grove, was poised over his squatting dog. Zimmer was missing most of his right arm; he gripped the leash with the other. A few months ago, Ray and his grandmother had been driving slowly over the dozen or so speed bumps in Coral Grove's parking lot. Ray saw Zimmer in the distance, walking his dog, gripping the leash as he was now with his left arm, the other one dangling like a fat happy thumb out of his shirt sleeve. Ray's grandmother had sped up, bypassed her parking spot, and circled around the lot. She rolled down the window and approached Zimmer from behind. "Bon jour, Mr. Zimmer." She waved to him out of the open window.

He took a step back, clearing his dog, who seemed to mimic Zimmer's befuddled expression, to safety. With his left hand, Zimmer choked up on the leash. Ray's grandmother was waving fanatically now. Zimmer smirked and raised his chin to acknowledge her, and she drove on. She rolled up the window, turned to Ray, and said, "He never waves."

Currently he approached Ray and his grandmother with his dog, a frantic white terrier who buried its nose in one of Ray's loafers, under the chair. "Tell me, Ray," he said. "Why don't I ever see you with a girl? When I was your age I seem to remember my grand-parents being far less interesting to me than girls."

Ray picked up the shoes and set them on his lap. "I guess when I'm your age I'll remember things differently then."

"I think your grandmother's warping you is what I think."

"Thoughts are very important," his grandmother said. "Thanks for stopping by."

Zimmer huffed and he and the dog moved on. Ray's grand-mother shifted her gaze to the parking lot, the rarely used Buicks and Lincolns whose rear windshields looked mahogany beneath the shaded carport. "If I had to tell the world one single thing," she said, "it would be, 'Go look for me somewhere else.'"

From the beginning to the end of her illness, his mother had had nearly two years to take him aside and share some final in-sight. Him sitting on the edge of her bed, holding her hand, the curtain closed. *I'm sorry to have to say this.* Or: *What I'm about to say might not make sense to you now.* Or: *This isn't going to be easy.*

"Are you okay?" Ray asked his grandmother. And then, to re-duce the broadness of the question—she hated broad questions—"Should we go back inside?"

"I'm fine. No, I feel remarkable right now. I feel like having breakfast for dinner." She smiled. "You look like you want to ask me something, Ray. Ask."

"You know what I want to ask you about."

"The rain in London? The price of tea in China?"

She had more. The dead soldier's canteen? The sleeves of my favorite vest?

He could tell that she had closed her eyes behind the sunglasses, something in the limpness of her smile. He wondered if she'd ever done something she didn't absolutely feel like doing. She always seemed comfortable, so exceedingly comfortable.

In Intro to Writing the teacher passed around lyrics to an Elton John song. "Poetry is mankind's rebuttal to sadness," he said very slowly, as if he'd just assembled the idea and needed to be careful with it while the glue dried. "Poetry," he repeated, waiting for everyone to take out his notebook, "is mankind's rebuttal to sadness."

He asked them to write an elegy, which they were to read aloud in class. Ray's was to an alligator he had watched a group of neighborhood kids lure from a lake and kill with aluminum bats. He'd started the poem as a joke, but soon found himself using up an afternoon figuring out how best to describe the alligator's gnarled legs. He wasn't about to eulogize his mother in front of his Intro to Writing class, but a dead alligator, a dead alligator was something he could pine for. Reading the poem aloud, he felt the easiness of insincerity. The rightness of meaning what you don't mean.

Dead on its back, its legs like unwanted souvenirs . . .

His teachers were fantastically serious. In Astronomy, the teacher asked questions like, "Now, what would happen if you accidentally steered your spacecraft into a black hole?" It was Ray's last class of the day, and the one that interested him least. "You'd totally die," was the correct answer, offered by one of the flip-flopping girls. Ray let the words fly past. Spacecrafts, black holes: certain things he had come to think of as impenetrable, pleasantly mystifying, and space was one of these things.

The girl in Astronomy who Ray remembered from high school asked one day after class, "Didn't your mom die or something?" She waited until he said yes to tighten her expression. "Sad," she said, as if to clarify the face she was making. When Ray got home, he looked through his yearbook and found the girl's picture in the Superlatives section. Most school-spirited.

One night, the class met on the roof of the GENED building and together watched the instructor aim his flashlight at the evening sky. The flashlight made for an ineffective spotlight; its beam disappeared a few yards above the building. "Cetus, Aries, Triangulum, Andromeda," he said. Then, extending his arm farther: "*There*, streaking meteors. There, do you see them? Right . . . *there?*"

Ray saw a sky the raw annulling color of deep water. It was full of distant holes of light traced by an airplane with its red beacon signal blinking. All of it so perfectly futile and lonesome—he shivered with self-pity. Away from Coral Grove, freed from his usual orbit, he wanted to remember this feeling. The sky offered nothing, and Ray offered nothing back. His mother was gone. He was alone, alone, alone. He sort of felt like howling.

Nobody else saw the meteors, so the teacher continued his incantation: Pegasus, Lacerta, Cepheus . . .

The wind picked up and Ray lowered his head. Most of his classmates were shivering where they stood, hugging themselves. One by one they began to go back downstairs, leaving the teacher and his flashlight, its feeble beam fanning out from his arm like a sneeze.

After class, Ray jogged to the bus stop, his loafers digging into his heels with each step. Out of breath, he approached the bench and saw, sitting on the far side, eyes closed, arms crossed, like something carved atop a sarcophagus, the girl with the baby. Tonight, though, she was without the baby. She wore a white jacket of puffed-out squares, zipped up to the neck. When Ray sat down she coughed and scooted over even farther. He waited for her to open her eyes, waited. Her hands were shaking. After a few minutes, he said, "How's your daughter?"

She jolted awake and looked over, clearly not remembering him, then shook her head. Her hair looked longer, curled out hopeful along her neck. "Deceased," she said.

The word came out assured and without accent. Ray waited for her to explain, then, thinking she must not have understood the question, repeated it.

"Something happen," she said. "Something slip in her lung and now she deceased."

The girl looked down at her knees, folded her hands, and shrugged her shoulders several times. After a few minutes Ray, trying to come up with something to say, realized she was crying. He moved closer and laid his hand on the shoulder of her jacket until the bus approached. Its headlights bounced and flared and made the night seem colder and darker. They sat down next to each other on one of the side-facing front seats. "Did you say Martha, or Marta, the last time I saw you?" he asked.

"I misunderstand."

"Your daughter. What was your daughter's name?" It seemed important that he know.

"Marta. She deceased two days. And now I misunderstand everything. The flowers man ask if I want rice at the funeral. The other man I think he say we should bury Marta in her diaper. I don't know what."

Her face tightened and she looked down and began shrugging her shoulders again, a dejected though modest movement. Ray found himself trying to remember what he could about the daughter, her warm, wilting hand, her dark eyes. As the bus rumbled past the girl's stop, she explained that she was headed to Sears to buy something for Marta to be buried in; she didn't know what children were supposed to be buried in.

"She too *small* to be deceased," the girl said. More shrugging, the jacket swishing against itself. Ray kept his hands in his lap.

"I'm sorry," he said.

"She not even sure what happen. She too small."

"I remember."

A few weeks ago, had he thought she was attracted to him? Had he imagined that when they met again he would ask her name and if she wanted to go see a movie? The idea seemed sort of vulgar now. The girl repeated, "She deceased two days."

He offered to go with her to buy the dress. Perhaps he expected her not to understand him, but she did, and her face brightened. He let his stop pass, feeling oddly watched and judged until his grandmother's condo was out of view. He noticed the mother had removed the gemstone from her nose; in its place was a tiny, tight puncture mark. Her name, she said, was Risa.

Sears was inside the older of the two malls in town, the mall preferred by panhandlers, graffiti artists, and Ray's grandmother. He hadn't been there since they went shopping for loafers more than a year ago. The inside smelled unequivocally like scorched hair. Most of the stores had shut down, replaced by little specialty kiosks in the center walkways. He and Risa walked past booths selling hermit crabs with brightly painted shells, cat calendars, personalized umbrellas, chair massagers, raffle tickets for skateboards and piñatas. In front of Sears, she handed him thirty-five dollars and said she wanted to wait outside.

Halfway into the lawn care section, he was approached by a saleswoman who said, "Cash money, cash money!" He was still holding the thirty-five dollars in his hand.

He turned around, walked out of the store, and found Risa sitting on the edge of a planter, beneath fake ferns that appeared to be browning. Her eyes were closed again and she looked forgone, defused. "Risa," he said. She opened her eyes slowly. "I don't even know what I'm supposed to buy. A dress?"

"Yes, right. A fancy." She held her arms out by her waist to indicate the desired puffiness of the dress.

"What size was Marta?"

"Nine months."

"No, size," he said. "How big was she?"

"Nine months."

She waited for the next question, her expression starting to go a little chaotic. Ray decided he'd figure out sizes in the store.

Finding a fancy dress was not difficult. The baby dresses were all frills and silk and velour, worn throughout the girl's section by doll-sized mannequins in frisky poses. "Baby's First Tea Party," one of them said. He felt obvious and corrupt, like a burglar shopping for ski masks. He grabbed the first shiny dress he saw, turquoise colored with white ruffles, on sale for $29.99. It seemed close to Marta's size. He hurried up and paid, not looking at the dress too carefully, trying to focus only on the transaction. Did he want the receipt in the bag? the cashier asked. An excellent question. Yes, yes he did.

"Um, I have doubts," Risa said after pulling the dress out of the bag, unable to conceal her disappointment. "Maybe some more big and warm, you know? With long sleeve?"

Ray waited, hoping she would notice his reluctance and change her mind. "Green maybe," she decided.

He walked back into the store with the bag and exchanged the dress for a new one, which was, according to Risa, too "itch-feeling." The next one was too cheap looking, and the one after that was no green, no green at all. Each time into the store he noticed details he'd managed to avoid the time before. The mother standing behind a toddler who gripped the edge of a grill to steady himself. The family looking politely miserable in the lobby of the portrait studio. The little boy asking his dad to buy him the T-shirt with the spiders on it.

By the fifth dress, he was annoyed with Risa, her clumsy English, the way she opened the bag and pulled out each dress, all greedy and doubtful. He tried to suppress the irritation—he had wanted to do the job solemnly for her, without complication—but she seemed to be punishing him. She had a long jawline and, through no fault of Ray's, was starting to resemble a coyote. "Are you sure you don't want to do this yourself?" he asked her. She was sure.

This time, when he brought the dress to the register, the cashier studied him suspiciously and said, "You need to go see Customer Service."

Take a left at Intimates, the cashier said, it's just across from Footwear.

The only thing that stopped him from going home right then and leaving Risa was the thirty-five dollars, a sum of money that, as he walked past racks of plus-size bras and camisoles, seemed tragic. Not quite twenty-five and not quite fifty. He knew he could forgive himself for not buying the dress she wanted; leaving with her thirty-five dollars, he decided, he couldn't.

He waited in line behind a woman with long purplish-gold hair extensions, who kept repeating, "How we gonna make this right?" to an attendant standing behind a window. Ray's feet hurt from walking so much. He had his back to the shoe section, but he knew that probably very nearby was a display with his loafers perched atop it.

The Customer Service attendant listened sympathetically to Ray's story and, when he was done, said to return the dresses as often as necessary. The man had a round heedful face, perfectly suited behind glass. "I hope this is the last time," Ray told him.

Risa's head was down and she was crying again when Ray came out of the store. Below her legs, just above the base of the planter, someone, Travis perhaps, had spray painted *Travis Owns the Vagina*.

"The world go on," she said when he sat down. "I see a baby look like Marta a lot. But Marta always stay how she is, you know? And all her *clothes*." Tears squirmed in the clumped mascara between her eyelashes. "I can't explain. I'm sad."

Ray handed her the bag and waited for her to open it. She set it down by her feet. "I buy a pretzel for you. Thank you."

She produced two pretzels, which she had enfolded in a series of napkins to keep warm. She handed him one, all swaddled in its wrapping. Seeing the care she had dispensed on it, he hesitated to eat it. It was encrusted with hot cinnamon sugar. After a few bites, he decided it was the best thing he'd ever tasted. "My mom died," he said when he was finished. It sounded a little more glee-ful than he intended, like bragging. Risa looked prepared to start crying again. "Over a year ago," he said.

"What is she like?"

He described a time at the health food store. He was bothering his mother to buy chewable vitamins or something, and she turned and, pretending not to recognize him, said, "And whose little boy are you?" This was a long time ago, when she was try-ing to lose weight with the Grapefruit 45 plan. Their shopping cart was filled with powder packets and mesh bags of citrus fruit, and she continued to repeat *whose little boy are you* as he fol-lowed her down the aisle.

At the time, he was more upset about being called a little boy than at the refusal to acknowledge him. For some reason the mem-ory was now stuck to her, sharp if not sweet, memorable if not sig-nificant. He liked remembering it. Every so often he'd be reminded of it, and the act of retrieval polished it to glistening again, for the next time. Describing it to Risa, he heard himself building to a punch line that never came.

"That's nice," she said, though Ray wasn't sure how much of it she understood. "I wish I could have more. Last night I try to count the baths she took."

The lights overhead dimmed and brightened, dimmed and brightened, signaling that the mall was about to close. "How many?" he asked.

"Twenty-nine," she said.

On the bus ride home, she held the Sears bag in her lap. She still hadn't opened it. Ray tried to recall what the dress looked like, and couldn't. The bus stopped every few blocks to pick people up; everybody seemed to be traveling with babies, but Risa appeared not to notice. "How is space?" she asked. She pronounced it *espace*.

The question surprised Ray, who said what he'd been thinking earlier on the roof: "Too big." A baby began crying nearby, an awful threshing cry, louder than the bus's loud heater. Risa peered around to see where it was coming from. And then, she pulled the cable at a different stop than the one at which she'd gotten off before, and thanked him again, kissing his cheek. An unreluctant kiss, startling and very agreeable. Her lips felt gummy and Ray knew he'd never see her again. She hugged the Sears bag against her white jacket. "This," she said, "means to me I can't say how much, you know?"

Looking at the empty seat where she had been, at the peach-shaped mark on the seat pad, Ray realized what she'd been referring to. Space. It was what he took up. He lay his forehead against the bus's window and let the vent blow into his eyes.

———

His mother, the last time he saw her, was almost unrecognizable, near bald, skinny, with dim green veins beneath her skin. The veins branched off and reconvened all over her neck and face, even on her closed eyelids, and were exhausting to look at. Get well cards sat open on one of the end tables, as well as a lone hardy jade plant that had outlasted all the floral arrangements. Machines monitoring her vital signs made doomed-sounding beeps, which didn't seem to alarm the nurses when they checked them. Ray sat near the door reading a celebrity-gossip magazine while his grandmother played solitaire on the other end table. She asked his mother, who was sleeping, if she remembered coming to bed with her when it started thundering. "You'd slide into bed between Poppy and me, and then out came the elbows."

Beep *bip* beep *bip*: two monitors were ticking at different speeds. Every minute or so the ticks would meet twice, then separate. His mother had become hypersensitive to contact and had stopped letting Ray and his grandmother touch her. The smell of her own teeth, she said, made her nauseous. Just thinking about sand in her panty hose was enough to make her gag.

"Like a swastika," his grandmother said, in such a way that Ray knew she was addressing him too. He looked up from the magazine. For weeks he'd been hoping his mother would make an announcement to him, something to mark her by. She continued to breathe damply. The machines continued monitoring.

"Time to go home," his mother said, then seemed to wake up. "I'm tired of being beheld."

"You don't mean that," his grandmother said.

"That's enough for today," she said. "It's selfish to bring him here every afternoon."

Ray had closed his eyes a while ago, but wasn't sleeping. If he opened them, his mother would look over and offer a pained smile, he knew it.

"I'd love it if people came and watched me for a few hours a day," his grandmother said. "I'd put on a show."

"I mean it, Mom. Take him someplace else. He has enough cancer memories."

"Foolishness. We'll let you rest. I'm sure you'll feel better in the morning."

This was the last time his grandmother brought him. A few days later they went to Sears. He knew she was buying the shoes for the inevitable funeral. As the salesman brought boxes of identical-looking loafers in and out of the storeroom, which were vetoed by either Ray or his grandmother, Ray tried to convince her that buying the shoes before his mother died was unfair, but that wasn't right. Unlucky? He didn't know the right word. His grandmother liked a pair of loafers with ludicrous jaunty tassels. "No one in those shoes needs to worry about a thing," she said.

"They look like golf shoes," he said.

Impatient, he agreed on the loafers and the salesman went to ring them up. Ray continued to protest. What if his mother found out what they had been doing? How would that make her feel? It seemed so . . . *disrespectful*. That was the word.

She waited for the salesman to reach the cash register, then turned to Ray and said, "She died, Ray. Yesterday, while you were in school."

She nodded to show him she wasn't joking, the gray braid sluggish along her shirt collar. He hated that she waited until they were in Sears to tell him. His mother had been sick for some time.

But Sears? At the register, the salesman held up the shoe box and shouted, "You wearing these out the store?"

"Are you serious?" his grandmother said. "I mean, imagine!"

———

At some point during the short walk from the bus stop to Coral Grove, which at night was lit from below like a monument by yellow floodlights, Ray decided to confront her. He was tired of pretending not to care about what his mother had said. He wanted his grandmother to tell him, no jokes, no stock phrases.

He found his grandmother in her bedroom. She lay in pajamas with her feet against the headboard, holding a paperback about a foot from her head, which rested flat on a quilt bedspread. She was wearing the prescription sunglasses. "Then Downtown Billy broke his leg, ending our father's dream of winning the Kentucky Derby," she read. "Trash, I spend my days deciphering trash." She put the book down and turned around to sit on the edge of the bed. "And I seem to have lost my eyeglasses." She took off the sunglasses and massaged her temples. The skin around her eyes strained and slackened.

"Judgment's stepson," she said. "I think I'll have some coffee before listening to what you surely have to say."

She went to the kitchen and turned on the faucet: Ray could hear the water pipes groaning between the walls. Her bedroom, without her in it, felt tiny. He wished he knew where Risa was going with the dress. *She too small to be deceased,* she had said. That word, said with such certainty, would never mean anything but the absence of Marta. A year from now, ten years.

"Change of venue," his grandmother hollered from the other room. He went into the dining room, where she was sitting in front of the hutch. She stirred a packet of instant coffee into a mug, looking intently at her hands. "I've been meaning to write a letter to Folgers. An appreciative letter."

"What did she say?" he asked. It came out lank and whiny. "No jokes. What did Mom tell you? I don't want to hear—"

"I know, Ray." She sipped from her coffee, then looked into the mug suspiciously. "You're trying to catch me off guard."

"Just tell the truth."

Her blue eyes scanned back and forth in their murk. Then she closed them and sighed. "In my thesaurus, there's a note between the flyleaf. Bring it to me."

The thesaurus was on the dressing table. He pulled out a green piece of paper with the familiar Mayo Clinic logo. *We Care and It Shows* was written beneath in soft script. The slogan was probably intended to soothe, but it had the reverse effect on him. Walking around the hospital while his mother was staying there, he would see the slogan everywhere, even on the cafeteria salad bar's plastic sneeze-guard. The more he saw it, the more he doubted it. Not the fact that they cared, or that it showed, but that it would make a difference.

The note, in his grandmother's handwriting, said: *I certainly wonder where I'm off to.*

"The day before your mother died," she said when he handed her the note. "She wanted me to write that down. I did, and there it is." She handed it back to him.

At first he thought she was playacting, but there was no spark in her expression. He read it again. In his grandmother's tight, angrily neat cursive it looked like scolding. He asked what his mother meant to say.

"Just that, I suppose. Maybe more. Definitely not less. I intended to add something to it, something remarkable, but I couldn't come up with anything. Then I thought about writing *I hope there are refreshments*, but." She paused to take a sip of coffee. "I didn't."

He stared at the note, then looked at her, huddled over her mug, wrapped in a lilac house robe. "You shouldn't have hidden this away like it was yours."

She didn't disagree. Nor did she wave him off with a rebuttal. Her mouth was half open, as if caught on a word. He stood next to the hutch, a punch away from all that etched crystal . . .

"It's a shabby message," she said. "The longer I waited to tell you about it, the shabbier it got. Of all the remarkable things she could have said."

"She said this."

"She could have said, 'No more buttoning and unbuttoning. I am happy now.' Or, 'Let us cross the river, Ray, and rest under the shade of the trees.'" He wasn't smiling. "You're right, I shouldn't have kept it."

"What does it mean?" His voice was squealing again, a little.

"A lot of nothing," she said. She watched him intently now. "She was sick, Ray. I'm sure she didn't know what she was saying. I bet it made absolute sense to her."

"You hid it in your thesaurus."

"I miss her, too," his grandmother said. "She was my good friend. I knew her all her life."

He sat down in a chair across the table from his grandmother and took off his shoes. His feet had begun to hurt again. "You know what?" he said, setting the shoes on top of the table. "I *hate* these shoes. I'm throwing them away."

"They're still fine shoes. At least give them to Goodwill."

"No one should be subjected to these shoes."

His grandmother, maybe sensing some levity, smiled and said, "Guess what we're having for dinner," but Ray wouldn't guess. Instead he stood up to go to his room, stopping first at the kitchen trash to throw away the shoes. His grandmother extended her hand when he passed, and he pumped it awkwardly, feeling her warm palm. "Just guess," she said. Her expression was agile, teasing. A burst blood vessel ran like a shrimp's mud vein down the length of her nose. Ray let go of her hand and went to his room.

What's for dinner, he would have asked her. Sleep, she would have answered.

He looked around his bedroom for a folder to put the note in. He wanted to save it for later, much later. He searched the drawers of his grandmother's old sewing machine, which he was supposed to be using as a desk. In one of them, beneath tangled spools and bobbins, he found a large photo of him and his mother. It was a posed portrait taken at the insistence of his grandmother a few weeks after his mother started chemotherapy. His grandmother had been asking them for years to have a formal photograph taken, preferably with an autumn theme. One afternoon, she drove them to the mall ("Ray needs school clothes"), brought them to the portrait studio, and wouldn't take no for an answer. Standing in front of a gold and russet backdrop, elbows on a fence post, his mother looked like a disgruntled scarecrow. Ray sat next to her, besieged by cowlicks, breakfast stains on the front of his shirt. Both of them frozen together by his grandmother in the wrong moment.

When his mother died, Ray thought the desolate feeling was at its worst, and its mildness surprised him. He had planned to cry, and he did, and to hurt for a while, and he did, and then to feel better. He figured her absence was a big hole that needed filling. But months passed and he missed her more, not less. Whenever some errant powder smell reminded him of her, he would realize that while her absence made the hole, her absence was also what came later to fill it.

At the sewing machine, he held on to the note and returned the picture to the drawer. He looked around his room for somewhere to put it. He went to his bed and decided to set it on top of the end table, against a porcelain lamp. He wanted the note to be there first thing when he woke up: the punch line, shouting its absence. He wanted to hear it.

The
Newcomer

<hr/>

In an airplane west across a wine-dark sea, Spiros travels to his new country. He is an inexperienced traveler and for now the gods look kindly upon him, blowing a gentle tailwind and seeing to it that he is seated next to one of the frank and wistful women he knows thrive where he is heading. She swallows a pill early in the flight, docks the knee of her long leg against his, and falls deeply asleep smiling. When the plane lands with a bounce in America she wakes up and smacks her lips. She has very satisfactory lips.

Spiros enrolls in the Institute for Advanced American Furtherance, a two-year academy advertised on the sides of buses in his old country. But he hasn't come to study; he is here to find women, the kind who respond to overtures only if properly set, in chartered villas and on the backs of motorcycles. At the Institute he spots one sunning herself on grass the custodians spray paint the color of welcome mats, and another on a bench loosening a grapefruit from its skin with a fatigued determination. Spiros is surprised by the variety: in his old country there was less variety. Though why don't these women associate with anyone? Why is their membership so scattered? He does not know. Maybe they are lonely.

Two weeks later he sits in the cafeteria of the Institute and watches bored women pass his table without a glance. There is nothing, he decides, as insistent as the nonglance of a bored woman. Today is Club Recruitment Expo Day and he tries to solicit their interest for Uh-oh, the national pastime of his old country. In front of him is a signup list and five-page explanation of the methods and protocol of international Uh-oh. On either side of him are other club representatives, to his left a man from the Pomeranian Re-enactors, and to his right a young woman from a group called People for the Ethical Treatment of Me. For international Uh-oh, a minimum of 202 participants are needed, half of them women. Currently on his signup list are only two signatures, his own and a bald Turk's from Spiros's Confronting Intermediate English class named Nuri Balicki. The young woman to his right chews her nails. Though she is not terribly pretty, neither frank-looking nor wistful, and a little undersized, she would make a perfect flank-side thunderer for Uh-oh, that is, one responsible for all the thundering done on the flank-side.

Spiros tells her this. She says, pulling the tip of her forefinger out of her mouth, "Who?"

"Uh-oh," he says. "The sport of besiege and capture between opposing sexes, and national pastime of my country, my old country. What number of signatures are on your list?"

"Four. Yours?"

"Two. I will tell you something. If you participate in Uh-oh club, I will in turn participate in this people for ethics group."

"PET ME."

"Soon enough."

"No, that's the name of my organization."

"Even so."

The fellow from the Pomeranian Re-enactors says, "Allow me to ratify this exchange with my presence and approval."

"What do the Pomeranian Re-enactors do?" asks the young woman.

"Besides reconstruct the sacred tours of Count Mieczislaw and Ladislaus II across wind-raked Pomerania, raising money for victims of domestic abuse along the way? Camp outdoors in the ancient mode. Venge, avenge. Tame steeds. Do either of you own a steed?"

Both shake their heads, one vigorously, the other not so.

"We'll have to find you some," says the Pomeranian Re-enactor.

When word of the exchange spreads through the cafeteria, representatives from the other clubs begin to approach one another with their signup sheets. Spiros makes sure everyone reads the many methods and protocol before they join Uh-oh. While they do, he signs up for the Gal Pals, Seeing-Eye Dog Liberation Society, Let's Rap!, Hadassah, People Oppressed By People Oppressed By People, Overeaters Anonymous, and several others he doesn't notice the names of. Many of the other club representatives say they are confounded by Uh-oh. The other club representatives have questions.

"What's the object of this game?" one asks.

"The object?" says Spiros. "What is the object of love? What is the object of stars locked in the sky? Of desire? Of constant crushing desire? Of really unmanning desire?"

"Can I bring my dog?" someone asks. "My dog helps me interact with people."

"Oppressor!" says the representative for the Seeing-Eye Dog Liberation Society.

"Oppressor!" answers the representative for People Oppressed By People Oppressed By People.

"He's strictly a leisure dog," the dog owner assures everyone.

"Uh-oh obtains its signification on the playing rink," Spiros says. "Then you will understand. But we still require about thirty women more."

The other club representatives watch this newcomer consider the problem of the needed players. Some of the club representatives, too, were once newcomers. They recognize the coiled intensity of purpose, the hint of cartoon zealotry in him, and recall the day theirs burned off. A few of them note the wand-shaped scar just above his jawline.

"I shall find a way," he says.

After the others leave, Spiros stays in the cafeteria and works in his Confronting Intermediate English textbook. Week three's exercise is *Joseph Anderson Admires the Seasons: Spring, Summer, Winter, Fall*, with photographs and short narratives for each season. *For Joseph Anderson, summer is a period of relaxation. Summer provides many hours of fun in the sun.* Joseph Anderson is a radiant force in bermuda shorts, an unbearably handsome man with that weary Western squint shielding the tangle of American nothingness behind his eyes. Spiros hates him and wonders what high-ranking government official this man must have wronged to find himself adorning the pages of a language textbook. *In the winter, Joseph Anderson enjoys the many excellent activities of the season. He skates on frozen lakes, skis in the snow, and sits in front of a hot fire.*

He writes, in his old language, *The wife of a high-ranking official should never outlive the delicateness of her desire,* trying to construct some sort of curt truth about wives.

He closes the textbook and sidearms it across the table. Yes, it will be necessary to round up some more women for Uh-oh. Their throbbing shoulder blades and painted toenails . . . nothing, nothing could be finer in the just-before-evening than a woman with painted toenails, hidden at the bottom of a pair of silk stockings like rubies in a satchel. Revelations—a word Spiros just learned—ten tiny revelations. Women are the only objects worthy of contained admiration, because they are never solved by it. Indeed, Spiros has begun to suspect that his admiration only complicates things. *He* desires *them,* but what do they desire? Him? Wealth? To further their personalities through idle chitchat? It's true, he knows very little about them. They have warped in these new surroundings, which more and more seem to him like a dream he will awake from back home in his old country, well rested, nostalgic, deluded. Like the old fisherman sitting over midday coffee at a café, whose boat and nets have been repossessed by the state bank. The fisherman has nothing now: his wife has left him. When she sees him at the café she spits in his direction and calls him *sourtani*, seat cushion. Day after day the fisherman plots schemes for buying back his boat, writing to friends and relatives to help him with some money for the creditors. He has tried to contact important men at the bank who don't return his calls and loaning agencies who do, telling him he has too unseemly a history. Once, the fisherman told Spiros that he didn't even like to fish or to sail! So why do you work to get back your boat? Spiros asked him. "My wife," the fisherman said. "She has the most astonishing talent . . ."

Meaning, exactly, Spiros thinks, what?

In the cafeteria, he overhears torn pieces of conversation, mostly students talking on cell phones explaining that they are talking on cell phones. He gathers his books and stands up to leave. At the table behind him, a student is coveting another's necklace aloud. He says, *I love gold link. I am* hard*core into gold link.* Not interesting! Everyone in the cafeteria, including Spiros, makes his hostile agreement with inactivity. A cell phone plays Yankee Doodle Dandy. One of the cashiers drops his head and sneezes loudly into his armpit. "Will someone turn off your phone," a woman says. "Somebody *please*, turn off your phone." Then, realizing it's her own, she reaches into her purse to answer it.

Ekaterina left her old country nearly two years ago on one of the Institute's student visas. In Kiev, the airport gate was crowded with soldiers and expectant travelers. The airport, large, disused, smelled of wet wool and oil. Leisure travel was a recent development. For Ekaterina, who had never flown in an airplane or been to Kiev before, every part of her passage revealed something unfamiliar. Rivers and hills dissolved to a white smear on the ascent, as the plane breached a dome of nacreous clouds. Some of the other passengers, unimpressed, had closed their window shades! Each time she transferred planes, she picked up souvenirs at the airport. In Zurich, she bought a dark-chocolate dog; in London, postcards depicting wooly-headed Parliament guards and double-decker buses. Once her plane landed in America, the candy was gone and the postcards written. A man from the Institute met her at the airport. He wore goggle-like glasses and a tattered leather jacket. Waiting for her luggage on the carousel, he kept pointing to bags, saying, "Sat it? Sat it?"

They pulled out of the airport in a white van.

"What do you plan on studying?" he asked once they were on the interstate.

She shook her head, feigning incomprehension.

"Take up? Study? Do you speak English?"

"Um, no?" she said.

He dismissed this by turning on the radio, flipping through the stations, and then turning it off again. He had the yellowish waxy hint of a beard, hair that looked pressed beneath lucid skin. "Can you say, tonight I will need to be fully touched?" he asked. "Or how about, my lap is moist?"

"Touch yourself," she said.

They drove into town. The man from the Institute tuned the radio to a pop music station and the two of them listened to a boy canting over a synthesizer. He looked at Ekaterina and snorted concisely, a laugh maybe. Once inside her new apartment, she sat on the carpet of the dim living room, her luggage still packed next to the front door, and waited for the landlord to turn on the power. There was a couch, end tables, a TV, a wicker chair, framed scenery prints. A dog howled from what sounded like inside her refrigerator. She felt lonesome. She began adding up everything she had witnessed so far that was new, a woman in the London airport with cheetah-print dyed hair, an obese toddler leashed to its mother, a billboard advertising a suicide hotline, a field of mangled yellow school buses under oaks hung with moss like the beards of saints . . .

Maybe ten minutes, maybe an hour later the TV turned on. Ekaterina opened her eyes to a woman listening to her toilet, which was moving its lid and seat like a mouth, saying it was a problem toilet, that it needed a problem-toilet disinfectant. Ekaterina turned off the TV and unpacked her bags.

Spiros walks around the Institute's campus, composed of a half-dozen identical coquina-shell buildings, each with a capital letter in its upper right corner and smoked black windows like hearses. The buildings give no hint of their age or of being mapped out and actually constructed. It is a place that seems to have simply occurred one day.

Between buildings, Spiros notices a yellow painted gazebo. As he moves closer, studying it with great curiosity and intent, he notices that it is filled entirely with young women he has never seen before. One, six, ten, twenty women at least, all holders of the same careless beauty. So *this* is where they congregate, this is the cathedral that celebrates frankness, carelessness. So many eyes and lips, how to depict them all? Each woman smokes a cigarette. Many wear sheer dresses with complex straps crisscrossing shoulder blades which, as the women bring the cigarettes to and from their lips, roll beneath sleek skin and look to Spiros like captive wings trying to break free. He feels a reverence for these tainted angels—yes, he will require them for his Uh-oh club, but he will not approach them yet. For now it will be sufficient to stay and witness them, and for them to blink and suspire, unaware of his urges. He thinks: Each woman, a controversy of abundance! We shall do more than watch one another! He thinks: Soon I will wear the marks of each gazebo angel's needs!

Now, it may be necessary to pause a moment and single out one of the gazebo women. How about Ekaterina, currently enrolled in the Institute's Practical Tactics program? She has a frail, vitamin-deficient look to her, with lazy deep-set blue eyes glowering downward like a cross but mostly innocent child. Much has changed in the two years since her passage. She has become steadily uninterested in the Institute and the prospect of furtherance or advanced furtherance. She is no longer homesick or lonely. She has only desire, slow, general, misplaced. She loves action movies and pop music. A man in her old country once told her she would make an exceptional archery target. The prospect of a fruitless life? This worries Ekaterina, indeed it worries most of the women at the smoking gazebo, not at all.

Ekaterina is unlike the rest of the gazebo women. They are citizens and she just a temporary visitor. Though she suspects they see her as an imposter and loathe her for it, assailing her when she is not around, she is wrong. Perception has never been required of them. Instead, they are content to be perceived, taken in by their classmates as brief quivers of perfect parts strolling to and from class, ranging but always returning to the yellow smoking gazebo. All, like Ekaterina, have flaws but none of them are particularly important. Only Ekaterina supposes that what's most palpable in their careless beauty is not beauty, but carelessness. Applause of cigarette-box packing, ripping of plastic film and paper, snip snip of lighters, exhalation. More pomp than circumstance, but such appealing, such well executed pomp. Let it be perceived.

———

"My esteemed homey," Nuri Balicki says at the Let's Rap! meeting. Spiros, who has come late, standing by the doors and waiting for his eyes to adjust to the room's dimness, failed to notice him there in the back row. "It is me, Nuri Balicki. Do you remember?"

"Confronting Intermediate English," Spiros says.

"Good, good. We are supposed to be pairing together now to collaborate on a rap hymn. I would very much like for you to be my copartner."

Spiros agrees. He sits down and together they compose a rap hymn on the subject of women. Nuri Balicki comes up with the chorus:

Me and you, girl, we can unh on a camelback, unh unh . . . unh.
Huh? you say to me. Talkin like a camel-hack, huh huh . . . huh?

He copies this onto a sheet of paper. When the Turk recites the *unh unh . . . unh* and the *huh huh . . . huh,* his wide chest shakes affably. His features are compressed, complex, and his skull has been shaved to the skin years ago at the onset of pattern baldness. Looking at the Turk's bare head, Spiros is reminded of that coarse American proverb: *I had to destroy the village to save it.* Many of the other club representatives from the Recruitment Expo are here at the meeting of Let's Rap! including the PET ME woman, the Pomeranian Re-enactor, the Dog Liberator—but not a single gazebo angel. They hide like oracles, acquiring significance in their refusal to participate. Right now they are probably nakedly sunning themselves behind a high wall or posing for an admirer's tattoo. Or overseeing a duel between frustrated suitors. Flourishing a scarf over the twin dueling pistols, shoulders flushed with ritual, the worm of longing shuddering through . . .

(Currently Ekaterina sits in a bathrobe in her living room, drinking wine and watching an action movie on television. The wife of the president has been abducted by a motorcycle group, and there are many high-speed chases. The secretary of state's limousine is driven off a cliff. The president declares, "They may have come here in peace—they'll leave in pieces!" and Ekaterina is able to apprehend the pun. She writes down new English words from the movie: *way-layed, scrou-up, mahshetty*. The wine is sweet, cheap, and she is extraordinarily comfortable, soothed by the slow click of the rotating ceiling fan. She begins to lose track where the commercials end and the movie begins. A bomb unit is dispatched, more problem toilets are cleaned. One of the motorcyclists is captured, a man in a cape wants you to know about Discount Furniture Kingdom, and a third paid too much for his fiancée's diamond-studded tennis bracelet. Confounding, but not at all disagreeably.)

Spiros turns to Nuri Balicki. "Do you know the women of the gazebo?" he asks. "Why are they none of them in extracurricular activities?"

"Oh yes-yes, the American *orospu*. These women are involved in thoroughly nothing but themselves. And themselves are nothing. So they are involved in nothing."

"Truly? But I cannot agree with you. Maybe they never feel welcome here. Maybe their scrawling country makes them uneasy. I plan to welcome them to my Uh-oh club. I must figure out a proper way for them to happily come and make themselves available."

"Maybe you should. Maybe you are right," Nuri Balicki says, clearly unconvinced. Then, adopting a more solicitous expression, he asks, "So what is your early opinion of your new country?"

"A chaos of ghosts—"

"Benevolent?"

". . . amongst beautiful women. It is what I always visioned."

"Oh, my homey, I think you are *far* too hasty," Nuri Balicki says. "In time you will reach a coherence in this new world, nearly everyone does. And then what? You will be angry that you ever resisted. No?"

"The only thing I will compile is American women. Do you think I traveled across the sea for a barbarous hamburger education?"

"Yes-yes. No. I think we must be from different viewpoints. Myself, I love everything of this country except the women. The women here are like cold . . . what's the English? . . . *sculptures.* Happily they have made a trade-in: style, yes please; character, no thank you."

"But you generalize."

"It is the Ottoman in me. I understand only on large scale."

"What are women in Turkey like?"

"Much the same, I am afraid. Nonetheless I am a fan of them. They have endeared themselves because of their, to me, familiarness. What it seems you are aspiring for in women is the opposite, the unfamiliarness. Is this a word? Oddity? Exotica? Yes-yes, you are an exemplary example of your country, an explorer, eager to celebrate newness and beautifulness, and wash out the low impulses in yourself and others. Probably I should talk less to you and listen more."

The two of them stand up. The Turk takes out a handkerchief to wipe the sweat from his forehead, above which runs a silhouette of less tanned skin like the shoreline of a dead sea. *I had to destroy it to save it.* Since his arrival in America, Spiros's sense of smell has been noticeably vitalized, and currently it picks up someone's sweet and intimate scent, a sort of personal syrup. A woman in the front of the room shouts, Let's rap! and Spiros begins to feel sick. There are times when he is exhilarated by the generosity of suggestion in his new country, the simple democracy of it, and times when it nestles its way into the piping of his chest and expires there. The Turk begins:

Hey, little angel, let me tell you what I think.
The two of us are in harmony, twin soldiers, when it comes to
beholding each other's juicy persons in the Uh-oh rink.

Exactly when the women moved in and claimed the gazebo as theirs, no one is sure. Early morning or in the evening, instantaneously or gradually over time, no one is sure. It was a bloodless coup, and the mortals were overthrown. The women now had a site to display themselves, listing over the gazebo rail in various tropisms, negligently blinking and breathing. The Institute's carpentry students, who never could have predicted their handiwork would house such luster, were asked to build a second smoking gazebo, which of course suffers in comparison. Students don't use it; even the Institute's birds and squirrels won't go near it. To lure them, the custodians have put stale bread and cake on the gazebo railing, but the animals remain in their trees, suspicious, chirping at the custodians who believe highly in and applaud this kind of discernment. "I don't blame them," the custodians say. "They know what they know."

The third smoking gazebo is an even larger disappointment. Someone has been using it, not one of the Institute's students or employees, it is hoped, as a toilet. High overhead in a blanched sky, a dozen or so buzzards circle it. Half of the gazebo is painted red because the carpentry students ran out of yellow partway through.

Classes are dismissed and the women come to light at the gazebo. Clap of packing, ripping of film and paper, snipping lighters, exhalation. The cigarettes are an imported type. The gazebo angels have no plans to quit.

How to recruit them?

For us to disentangle the route to which Spiros arrives at his decision of how, exactly, to induce the gazebo women to participate in the inaugural meeting of Uh-oh, to mark his doubt, perplexity, and relief, the guilelessness with which he finally arrives at a method— a very traditional one, by the way, though Spiros doesn't realize this, because in all his years practicing the sly diplomacy of direct romantic pursuit he has never employed it—would be tedious. He decides to be straightforward with them.

Let us join them mid-conference, Spiros standing outside the gazebo looking in with his right hand shielded over his eyes, thumb on temple, as if in prolonged salute to the gazebo angels.

". . . but I told him it is thought by me," he concludes. "That this is not the case."

He was referring to the earlier conversation with the Turk, which he has tried to re-enact for the women. They have been listening, he can tell from the way they have allowed their cigarettes to smolder between their fingers. "Where are you from?" one of them asks.

Spiros says, "Did you ever read *the wine-dark sea?*"

Cigarettes still smoldering, no response from the women.

"Well, this is my old country."

This close, he can better form assumptions about each of them. The one who asked where are you from wears a black dress with an egg-shaped aperture at the midriff exposing a tan, very satisfactory midriff. She is stern but curious, unconstrained, navigable, available to be compiled.

"You say we conduct the initiatory charge, but what does the winner get? What is the object of this Uh-oh?"

"The object?" says Spiros. "What is the object of love? What is the object of desire? Of constant crushing desire? Of really unmanning desire?"

"Of the thirst that has no new name?" one says.

"Of the loneliness mistakes make?" another says.

Desirous, desirous, desirous, available to be compiled. "Beautiful! You see!" he says. "You surely must have somewhere played Uh-oh before."

"Of phone conversations missing things?" (This is said by Ekaterina.)

"Please, that's enough," the one with the very satisfactory midriff says. "We'll talk this over and let you know."

"Of course, of course. I leave you with a description of protocols and list of possible uniforms and strategy, and tell you we play a fortnight from Wednesday at four o'clock."

Spiros walks away from the gazebo, hearing the lazy suspiration, the affirmative whispers of the angels. He has been hallowed in their cigarette fumes—as he passes a group of carpentry students, he can smell the dowdy smoke, pulled by the angels' lips, past teeth, tongues, tonsils, tracheas, bronchia, and held, caressing their pleura and alveoli, briefly, before it was released, all over his clothes and skin. An intimate exchange between the women and him, far more pleasing in memory than in act, like most intimate exchanges. A petting zoo of urges! Together they shall soon yoke! An intimate exchange, far more pleasing in anticipation than in memory, like most intimate exchanges.

The carpentry students are at work on a fourth gazebo, debating whether they should theme this new structure a smoking gazebo like the others, or a smoking bower, smoking hogan, smoking temple, smoking grotto, smoking hermitage, smoking sanctuary, or smoking retreat. It is finally decided to theme it orientally, with scrolls and characters, dragons, tigers, maybe buy some gold paint and finish out the red, and plant bamboo around it for maximum theme. This one they will call a smoking pagoda. The night before they plan to cut the ribbon and grand-open it, someone, not one of the Institute's students or employees, it is hoped, will pour flammables on it and burn it down to an octagonal patch of concrete and ash. Over which the buzzards, even the buzzards, will hesitate to fly.

Often Ekaterina wonders when she will begin feeling homesick. She now loves a third thing, besides action movies and pop music—Boone's Farm wine, which she buys at Qwik Stop, near her apartment. Always there seem to be the same twelve people lined up in the car parts aisle waiting to trade in to the cashier pink and white lotto forms. They mark the forms with stubby pencils, using fashion magazines and cereal boxes for leverage, and look suspicious to her, not themselves guilty, but suspicious of everyone else in line. She tries to ignore their stares and enjoy the popular sounds of Boyzterious playing on her headphones. Boyzterious, the conjunction of boyz and mysterious, is her favorite music group. They are on a mission, according to their liner notes, to lighten the vicissitudes of existence with funky beats and jams. Most important to know, they are four boyz who are, each one of them, mysterious. For instance, they are not boyz at all, but forty-year-old men with high-school-age children and prostate anxiety. One of the boyz likes to wear humorous caps. Another has a grayish braided goatee he wants to sing you a song about and, what's more, which you want to hear a song about, and all of it is extremely mysterious.

The Qwik Stop cashier says, "Sup," nods, and winks his right eye all in a single ostentatious movement, which Ekaterina practices on the walk home.

Once a week, she talks to her family on the telephone, hearing the old sounds in the background as her younger sister goes on about a boyfriend: kitchen clatter, voices clamoring over politics on the radio, her dog barking. "Do you not think he sounds appealing?" her younger sister asks. "Tell me, does Tiger Woods live near you?" She hands the phone to their mother. "How is our modern Ukrainian woman of the United States?" she asks. She is washing dishes; Ekaterina recognizes the caustic fizzing sound of the sanitation tablets, which her mother still uses even though they've had hot water for nearly a decade. When Ekaterina tells her she has signed up for the Institute's Uh-oh club, her mother says, "A veritable American!" then asks, "Uh-oh is game show?" She hands the phone to Ekaterina's father. "When will you be finished with your schooling and return home to us?" he asks.

Off the phone, she makes dinner for herself, a chipped beef boil-in-bag served on toast and a handful of miniature carrots.

She watches a repeat of the movie about the kidnapped president's wife. It makes less sense to her the second time. During a commercial, a talking dog wants her to be sure to buy special Christmas Dog Chow this holiday season. He sits on an ottoman, gesturing frantically with his front paws, and his mouth moves. There is something calming to Ekaterina in the satisfied smile of a dog, his visible optimism and perfectly articulated appetite, pointing out that he needs lutein as part of a balanced diet and he needs bigger Christmas taste. Seeing him, she too feels satisfied, though she has no reason to be, except maybe the wine. This is not her home, why isn't she homesick? She is alone, why isn't she lonely? The satisfaction, the undue optimism: she wants to stay in her new country forever or, failing that, until Boyzterious releases several more recordings. Ekaterina's unease is slight and seldom: once a week, after she has talked to her family on the telephone.

In the morning, the only thing troubling her is the certainty that nothing is troubling her.

Spiros walks to class from his apartment, a journey which leaves him feeling resigned and mildly glad, until he catches sight of the industrial-beige buildings of the Institute, the smoked windows. As he approaches them, they don't slowly come into view like a vista—they seem to *grow*. A custodian in a golf cart passes by, tweezing with giant metal tongs Diet Sprite cans and fast food wrappers off the ground and deftly tossing them into the back of the cart. In the shadow between two buildings, two boys slouched over bongos bang arhythmically to the delight of a few sandy-haired girls who laugh and scribble graffiti into the benches they are sitting on. The girls look florid, drugged, capsized.

Today the yellow smoking gazebo is empty of angels, a sign interpretable by Spiros as either encouraging or discouraging. On one hand, they could be preparing their uniforms for today's match, fashioning the necessary body trinkets as outlined by the protocols of international Uh-oh. Or convening to talk strategy for their initiatory, a movement most important, push. Another possibility is that they are embarrassed to cross paths with him again and have decided to permanently sequester themselves in order to maintain their honor. Spiros moves past the gazebo, smelling the smoke and floral smell to which he has come to connect the women. He hadn't considered the prospect of them not showing up and now that he does, he feels the idea unfold, then relax into his memory, assuming a sluggish inevitability. Minus the angels, the gazebo looks like a cheap lawn oddity. Spiros feels a pain in his stomach, as the smell of lunch wafts down from the cafeteria. Dry leaves ride along the red-ant mounds that skirt the gazebo, over tidy rows of stabbed cigarette butts that look like ant stovepipes or ant memorials.

Spiros has been in America thirty-eight days. He has learned that a quality, preowned sofa is actually a used sofa; that all three words in Kash N' Karry, the supermarket he uses, are misspelled; and that the women here, though far more assorted and plentiful, resist compilation as quietly yet resolutely as they did in his old country. The days waiting for the first Uh-oh match, with the exception of the brief exchange with the gazebo angels, have been filled with frustration and doubt. The former is familiar; the latter, not too.

"Would you like I bring you to dinner?"

No, they say.

"Are you as full of bubbling longing as the cinema actress you resemble?"

No, they say.

"Do the gods know your eyes are handsome stars?"

No. Drawing out the vowel, an accidentally sensual *ohhhhhh*.

Their blunt refusals both speak directly to him and beyond him. They are intimate and impersonal, authentic and generic, like the commercials on television telling him to buy an Aerobicizer, eat more pork loin, reinvent yourself in Virginia Beach, at the same time saying: what you have is unsatisfactory and what you long for is probably too large. The symbolic castle of want is surrounded by a symbolic moat stocked with chomping symbolic alligators . . .

A final view of Ekaterina:

At the bathroom mirror, studying her own lazy eyes lazily. They are her most notable feature, meant to view and be viewed simultaneously. Their hazel-splashed irises, brilliant under the bald fluorescent tubelight, watch her fingers slide pins into her hair. Her hands are always reaching toward hair, headphones, cigarettes, remote control, telephone. Everything so accommodating, pleasing, easy, worthwhile, briefly.

She steps back from the mirror, admires herself in full armor. Her eyes make a little agreeable gesture.

How fair! she says. How fresh! she says.

And is convinced, briefly.

Out of the 101 male participants who signed up for Uh-oh, only Spiros and Nuri Balicki make it to the Institute's field for the inaugural meeting, and only Spiros wears the prescribed armor. A gift from his father, black and heavy as a cast-iron skillet, it accepts all of the late afternoon sun's heat, causing him to sweat liberally from multiple ports. The ground is covered with a mousy-smelling mist.

The Turk stares down at it in his denim torn shorts and T-shirt depicting a beer slogan.

"To begin we use sheep's knuckle to see who leads the initiatory push," Spiros says. "But due to a large show of atheism by our fellows, you and I will alone lead."

"But the men, the women, none has showed up." The Turk beckons halfheartedly to the open field. "Hey, why don't we call this off and go to a local café and converse."

"*We* are the men's team," Spiros says. "The women's team is plotting to overtake us. We must instead overtake *them*, you see. It is matter of governance, of tradition, of desire, of fierce really unmanning desire . . ."

He had planned a rousing speech for the gathered horde. Instead, he points to the kudzu-covered bluff at the edge of the field. "We will begin there."

"This is foolish. I feel sorry for us."

"Uh-oh is a game of initiatory and retaliatory pushes. It perfectly mimics, and often leads to, the sex act."

"Right now my ancestors are weeping in their ziggurats," the Turk says.

The Turk and Spiros walk toward the bluff, beads of sweat forming atop the dead sea of the Turk's skull. Spiros's armor makes a gritty, not a clanging sound, as he always expects it to. Once, his father told him the armor dated back to a time when Uh-oh was waged in their country as a battle between opposing religions and was known as The Crusades. In the past century, pursuit of God, his father said, had given way to pursuit of available women by men, available men by women, with variation, and the world was more habitable because of it. This was one of the old man's considerable lies, Spiros now realizes. An impulsive and talented liar, he was, confusing the world around him, he said, to make it more interesting.

Noticing Spiros's wistful expression, the Turk asks, "Are you still missing your old country?"

"I am every day missing less and less. Now only I am missing when I missed it before, do you see?"

"Yes-yes, my esteemed homey, I do exactly see. Sometimes it is the opposite situation with me. I miss what I yet have not lost.

You, for instance. I am missing you already. And I am missing the you that misses when he used to miss. I miss that soon you will not miss."

And then, all at once on the tip of the bluff, the jagged outline of the gazebo angels appears to the two men. Motionless in their homemade armor, rising from the kudzu densely and lushly like overgrowth, the angels shine and loom, pompous with intent. The ground mist evaporates beneath Spiros's shoes. Some of the women have wrapped their top halves in aluminum foil, giving the illusion of the crystalline cap of a wave soon to break. Their helmets are festooned with gilded smoking charms, specially made holders for their burning cigarettes. Some hold coiled ropes, lengths of wood, croquet implements, all banned. One of them improvises a battle moan. The Turk responds with a hyperventilated expletive. Spiros's notice convenes on the forwardmost angel, looming in painted bronze, Ekaterina. Her appearance seems uncharacteristic, gate-opening. She is tall. There is a fellowship in her sunken eyes, a surfeit of misunderstanding like his own, as she raises her arm and gives the command, the loveliest phrase in her American vocabulary, *Forward!*

"What do you say to this?" Spiros asks the Turk.

"Uh-oh," Nuri Balicki says.

A flash of breasts in thin foil, very satisfactory midriffs painted like bright wartime pennants, tan lines revealed, Ekaterina still ahead of the lush tumble of inhibitions down, down the bluff. Like a press of errant bees! Like a press of errant bees!

"Exactly," Spiros says.

THE IOWA SHORT FICTION AWARD AND JOHN SIMMONS SHORT FICTION AWARD WINNERS, 1970–2006

Donald Anderson
Fire Road
Dianne Benedict
Shiny Objects
David Borofka
Hints of His Mortality
Robert Boswell
Dancing in the Movies
Mark Brazaitis
The River of Lost Voices:
Stories from Guatemala
Jack Cady
The Burning and Other
Stories
Pat Carr
The Women in the Mirror
Kathryn Chetkovich
Friendly Fire
Cyrus Colter
The Beach Umbrella
Jennifer S. Davis
Her Kind of Want
Janet Desaulniers
What You've Been Missing
Sharon Dilworth
The Long White
Susan M. Dodd
Old Wives' Tales
Merrill Feitell
Here Beneath Low-
Flying Planes
James Fetler
Impossible Appetites
Starkey Flythe, Jr.
Lent: The Slow Fast
Sohrab Homi Fracis
Ticket to Minto: Stories
of India and America
H. E. Francis
The Itinerary of Beggars

Abby Frucht
Fruit of the Month
Tereze Glück
May You Live in
Interesting Times
Ivy Goodman
Heart Failure
Ann Harleman
Happiness
Elizabeth Harris
The Ant Generator
Ryan Harty
Bring Me Your Saddest
Arizona
Mary Hedin
Fly Away Home
Beth Helms
American Wives
Jim Henry
Thank You for Being
Concerned and Sensitive
Lisa Lenzo
Within the Lighted City
Renée Manfredi
Where Love Leaves Us
Susan Onthank Mates
The Good Doctor
John McNally
Troublemakers
Kevin Moffett
Permanent Visitors
Rod Val Moore
Igloo among Palms
Lucia Nevai
Star Game
Thisbe Nissen
Out of the Girls' Room
and into the Night
Dan O'Brien
Eminent Domain

Philip F. O'Connor
  Old Morals, Small
  Continents, Darker Times
Sondra Spatt Olsen
  Traps
Elizabeth Oness
  Articles of Faith
Lon Otto
  A Nest of Hooks
Natalie Petesch
  After the First Death
  There Is No Other
C. E. Poverman
  The Black Velvet Girl
Michael Pritchett
  The Venus Tree
Nancy Reisman
  House Fires
Elizabeth Searle
  My Body to You
Enid Shomer
  Imaginary Men
Marly Swick
  A Hole in the Language
Barry Targan
  Harry Belten and the
  Mendelssohn Violin Concerto

Annabel Thomas
  The Phototropic Woman
Jim Tomlinson
  Things Kept, Things
  Left Behind
Douglas Trevor
  The Thin Tear in the
  Fabric of Space
Laura Valeri
  The Kind of Things
  Saints Do
Anthony Varallo
  This Day in History
Lex Williford
  Macauley's Thumb
Miles Wilson
  Line of Fall
Russell Working
  Resurrectionists
Charles Wyatt
  Listening to Mozart
Don Zancanella
  Western Electric